D0369708

G. K. CHESTERTON:
THE APOSTLE OF COMMON SENSE

DALE AHLQUIST

G. K. CHESTERTON: THE APOSTLE OF COMMON SENSE

IGNATIUS PRESS   SAN FRANCISCO

Cover design by Roxanne Mei Lum

ISBN 0–89870–857–5
Library of Congress Control Number 2002112866
Printed in the United States of America ∞

To My Parents

who first taught me what Chesterton
only confirmed,
that
"Thanks are the highest form of thought."

CONTENTS

PREFACE

There are some people who for some reason think it is pretty funny that I read my first Chesterton book while I was on my honeymoon and that the name of the book was *The Everlasting Man*—and that my bride was reading *Les Miserables*. Really.

The Everlasting Man may not be the best first book to read after getting married, but it is also not the best first book to read by Chesterton. Except that there is no best first book to read by Chesterton. Whatever book one chooses to read first, it seems it would have been better to have read one of the others first. Or several of them.

Still, you have to start somewhere, because not to read G. K. Chesterton is simply to cheat yourself of the incomparable experience of entering a world that is more invigorating and refreshing and awe-inspiring and complete than anything created by any other writer of the last century. By the time you read your third or fourth book by Chesterton, you will find that you have gotten past the problem of reading the first one.

While the perfect introduction to the marvelous GKC will likely elude us a bit longer, I am hoping this book may fill the need in the meantime. It arose from a television series I hosted that was created to introduce people to Chesterton. It is designed only to whet the appetite, but with Chesterton it is easy to fill up on appetizers. And perfectly acceptable.

And while this book focuses more on Chesterton's Catholic and Christian writings than on his novels or poetry or literary criticism, this serves to give a useful perspective for the rest of his writings. The tales are told one by one, but every single idea is inextricably connected to every other idea. No matter what you choose to say about Chesterton, you will necessarily leave something else out; but whatever the case, his faith is not something that can be ignored. It is not just one aspect of his work. On the contrary, it is "the great dome over all". It is the place to begin and end. After all, nothing makes sense unless everything makes sense.

I would like to thank Steven Beaumont and all the folks at Eternal Word Television Network for doing such an excellent job of bringing the Chesterton series to life, which in turn made this book possible. Thanks, too, to John Peterson, Chestertonian extraordinaire and world's greatest expert on Father Brown, for his help not only with the Father Brown chapter but for his years of gathering great quotations when he edited the *Midwest Chesterton News*. Gratitude also to the wizard Peter Floriani, without whom I would still be looking up references. And I could not have accomplished any of this without the unending love and support of my wife, Laura, and my children, Julian, Ashley, Adrian (whose middle name is Chesterton), Sophia, and Landon.

The most special thanks go to Chuck Chalberg, the "Man Who Was Chesterton" in the series and who contributed so vitally to every page. His talent is matched only by his humility. I will never forget the fact that when I was writing the scripts in which he would portray G. K. Chesterton, he actually worried that he was getting all the good lines.

I

An Introduction to
the Apostle of Common Sense

The most dangerous thing in the world is to be alive; one is always in danger of one's life. But anyone who shrinks from that is a traitor to the great scheme and experiment of being.

—"What Is Right with the World"

One scholar called him "one of the deepest thinkers who ever existed."[1] One pope called him a gifted defender of the faith.[2] One of his greatest opponents said the world is not thankful enough for him.[3] He was recognized everywhere he went and loved by everyone who knew him. He was a

[1] Étienne Gilson, renowned Thomist scholar, quoted in Maisie Ward, *Gilbert Keith Chesterton* (New York: Sheed and Ward, 1942), 620.

[2] Pope Pius XI, upon the death of Chesterton in 1936, quoted in Ward, *Chesterton*, 652. Ironically, the British newspapers would not print the tribute because the title "defender of the faith" had been bestowed on Henry VIII by Pope Leo X.

[3] George Bernard Shaw, in a review of Chesterton's book *Irish Impressions*, reprinted in D. J. Conlon, ed., *G. K. Chesterton: The Critical Judgments (1900–1937)* (Antwerp: Antwerp Studies in English Literature, 1976), 363.

master of the written word, a poet, a philosopher, a literary critic, a debater, a journalist, and a champion of social justice. What is he best remembered for? His detective stories.

Let us start by getting something straight: G. K. Chesterton was the best writer of the twentieth century. He said something about everything, and he said it better than anybody else. He was incredibly prolific. And incredibly profound. His prose was poetic, and, unlike most modern poetry, his poetry was also poetic. He was intuitive, incisive, and besides that, he was funny. To read him is to enjoy him.

But hardly anyone reads him anymore. He is the most unjustly neglected writer of our time, and we neglect him at our peril.

Chesterton is no longer taught in schools, but students should not consider themselves educated until they have read him. Furthermore, reading Chesterton is almost a complete education in itself. He covered all the bases. Art and literature. History and philosophy. Economics and social reform. Religion and politics.

Why is Chesterton neglected? Because the modern world finds it much more convenient to ignore him than to risk engaging him in an argument, because to argue with Chesterton is to lose. Chesterton argued eloquently against materialism and scientific determinism, against relativism, agnosticism, atheism, and other diseased philosophies that have infected the halls of academia for more than a century. He also argued against both socialism and capitalism and showed why both have been the enemies of freedom and justice in modern society.

And what did he argue *for*? What was it he defended? He defended the ordinary man. He defended the family. And he defended the Catholic faith. Perhaps that is why he is neglected. The modern world prefers writers who excuse sin, who scoff at Christianity, who deny the dignity of the poor, and who think freedom means no responsibility.

In 1905, a famous London newspaper, the *Illustrated London News*, hired Chesterton to write a weekly column. He was told he could write about anything he wanted—except religion and politics. Chesterton responded by saying there was nothing else worth writing about. As he would later observe,

> Religious liberty might be supposed to mean that everybody is free to discuss religion. In practice it means that hardly anybody is allowed to mention it.[4]

Chesterton went ahead and wrote the column for the next thirty years, and every week he wrote about religion and politics. He never backed away from controversy, but if you think about it, every controversy, every argument, every discussion is really about religion or politics. Or both. Religion has to do with our relationship with God. Politics has to do with our relationship with our neighbor. These are controversial for the simple reason that all the problems in the world come from our failure to obey the two great commandments: to love God and to love our neighbor.

> The Bible tells us to love our neighbours, and also to love our enemies; probably because they are generally the same people.[5]

Chesterton was controversial, and still is, because he took the trouble to defend simple, basic truths. The First Things. The Permanent Things. In spite of what the newspapers say, in spite of what the colleges teach, and in spite of what laws

---

[4] *Autobiography*, in vol. 16 of *The Collected Works of G. K. Chesterton* (San Francisco: Ignatius Press, 1987), 225. (Hereafter citations from the *Collected Works* will be abbreviated as *CW*, followed by volume number: page number.)

[5] *Illustrated London News* (hereafter *ILN*), July 16, 1910, *CW* 28:563.

the politicians make, most people hold certain basic truths in common. Chesterton said that the common things are not commonplace; they "are terrible and startling, death, for instance, and first love".[6] The common things are the basis of common sense. Chesterton called common sense "that extinct branch of psychology".[7] In the modern world, common sense and the common man are under constant attack.

> Modern emancipation has really been a new persecution of the Common Man. If it has emancipated anybody, it has in rather narrow ways emancipated the Uncommon Man. It has given an eccentric sort of liberty to some of the hobbies of the wealthy and to some of the lunacies of those who call themselves cultured. The only thing that it has forbidden is common sense, as it would have been understood by the common people.[8]

In this book, we are going to take a look at Chesterton's message for the modern world and see why he can be called the Apostle of Common Sense. But first, let us learn a little more about the man himself.

Gilbert Keith Chesterton was born in England in 1874 and died in 1936. He never went to college; he went to art school. In 1900, he was asked to contribute a few magazine articles on art criticism, and he then went on to become one of the most prolific writers of all time. He published over fifteen million words. He wrote a hundred books, contributions to two hundred more, hundreds of poems and short stories, including, of course, a popular series of mysteries featuring the priest-detective Father Brown. Though he wrote

---

[6] *Charles Dickens, CW* 15:179.

[7] *Sidelights, CW* 21:507.

[8] *The Common Man* (New York: Sheed and Ward, 1950), 1.

in nearly every literary genre, he considered himself primarily a journalist. He wrote over four thousand essays for several London newspapers. And he edited his own paper, *G. K.'s Weekly*, for the last eleven years of his life. He was a popular lecturer and debater in his time, taking on such contemporaries as George Bernard Shaw, H. G. Wells, Bertrand Russell, and Clarence Darrow. He traveled to several countries in Europe and twice to the United States on lecture tours.

G. K. Chesterton was a giant. In every way. A massive mind in a massive body. He stood at a towering six feet, four inches, and he weighed three hundred pounds. His weight was the subject of many jokes, most of which he told himself. For instance, he said he was one of the most polite people in England. After all, he could stand up and offer his seat to *three* ladies on a bus.

Certainly he was recognized wherever he went. One young woman said to him, "Everybody seems to know you, Mr. Chesterton." To which he sighed, "If they don't, they ask."

It is not hard to understand why everyone recognized him. In order to keep him somewhat tidy, his wife dressed him in a huge cape and wide-brimmed hat. The giant made his way down the street, squinting through tiny glasses pinched on his nose, blowing laughter through his moustache and a cloud of smoke from his cigar. He also carried a swordstick. Yes, the sword was real, but he was never known to use it except to stab at the pillows in his study while he dictated an essay or a book chapter. In his youth he had also carried a gun. He had never been known to use that either. Except, he claimed, when he heard someone say that life was not worth living. Then he would take out the gun and offer to shoot the person, "and always with the most satisfactory results".[9]

_____

[9] *ILN*, March 17, 1906, *CW* 27:144.

A selection of his quotations demonstrate his joy and wonder at life:

The supreme adventure is being born.[10]

Existence is still a strange thing to me; and as a stranger I give it welcome.[11]

We should always endeavour to wonder at the permanent thing, not at the mere exception. We should be startled by the sun, and not by the eclipse. We should wonder less at the earthquake, and wonder more at the earth.[12]

The test of all happiness is gratitude.[13]

Thanks are the highest form of thought.[14]

You say grace before meals.
All right.
But I say grace before the play and the opera,
And grace before the concert and pantomime,
And grace before I open a book,
And grace before sketching, painting,
Swimming, fencing, boxing, walking, playing, dancing;
And grace before I dip the pen in the ink.[15]

Chesterton was a marvelously clear thinker, but he usually had no idea where or when his next appointment was. He did much of his writing in train stations, since he usually missed the train he was supposed to catch. He once hailed a cab to take him to an address that turned out to be across the

[10] *Heretics, CW* 1:143.
[11] *Autobiography, CW* 16:329.
[12] *ILN,* October 21, 1905, *CW* 27:41.
[13] *Orthodoxy, CW* 1:258.
[14] *A Short History of England, CW* 20:463.
[15] Ward, *Chesterton,* 61.

street. And he once sent a telegram to his wife that read, "Am at Market Harborough. Where ought I to be?"

His absent-mindedness may have been legendary, but his present-mindedness may have been even more so. He could actually write out an essay in longhand, while at the same time dictating a different essay to his secretary.

This absent-minded, overgrown elf of a man, who filled up a room when he entered it, who laughed at his own jokes and would amuse children at birthday parties by catching buns in his mouth, this was the man who wrote a book that led a young atheist named C. S. Lewis to become a Christian.[16] This was the man who wrote a novel that inspired Michael Collins to lead a movement for Irish independence.[17] This was the man who wrote an essay in the *Illustrated London News* that inspired Mohandas Gandhi to lead a movement to end British colonial rule in India.[18] This was the man who wrote a book on Charles Dickens that is widely considered the best book ever written about that great author.[19]

When Chesterton burst upon the literary scene, he impressed readers and critics with his brilliant wit, his matchless style, and his artful use of paradox.

A citizen can hardly distinguish between a tax and a fine, except that the fine is generally much lighter.[20]

---

[16] The book was *The Everlasting Man*. See C. S. Lewis, *Surprised by Joy* (New York: Harcourt Brace Jovanovich, 1955), 190–91.

[17] The novel was *The Man Who Was Thursday*.

[18] The column appeared in the *Illustrated London News*, October 2, 1909. The account is described in Alzina Stone Dale, *The Outline of Sanity: A Life of G. K. Chesterton* (Grand Rapids, Mich.: Eerdmanns, 1982), 137–38.

[19] Among those who held this opinion were T. S. Eliot, William James, Theodore Roosevelt, André Maurois, George Bernard Shaw, and Dickens biographer Peter Ackroyd.

[20] *ILN*, May 23, 1931, *CW* 35:524.

Men do not differ much about what things they will call
evils; but they differ enormously about what evils they will
call excusable.[21]

A new philosophy generally means in practice the praise of
some old vice.[22]

It is not always wrong to go to the brink of the lowest prom-
ontory and look down on hell. It is when you look up at
hell that a serious miscalculation has probably been made.[23]

Take away the supernatural, and what remains is the
unnatural.[24]

Critics were amused by his epigrams and his paradoxes. And
though he seemed to be defending the Christian faith, they
assumed he was doing it merely for effect. But when they
found out that he was defending it because he actually believed it and not just for its shock value, they were, well,
shocked.

In 1922, they were shocked even more, however, when
G. K. Chesterton joined the Roman Catholic Church. That
a great man of letters should embrace the ancient Church of
Rome was something of a scandal in the literary world and
the intellectual establishment. They thought that Chesterton had suddenly become narrow, when in fact, he became
universal. What for them was a complete puzzle was for Chesterton himself the final piece of the puzzle, the completion
of a complete thinker.

---

[21] *ILN*, October 23, 1909, *CW* 28:413.
[22] *ILN*, January 6, 1906, *CW* 27:98.
[23] *Alarms and Discursions* (New York: Dodd Mead, 1911), 29.
[24] *Heretics*, CW 1:88.

It cannot be emphasized enough that Chesterton was a complete thinker. That is why he is such a challenge to the modern world. We have come to prefer incomplete thinking. We want things in fragments. That way we do not have to think about our inconsistencies. That way we do not mind when our jobs contradict our ideals, or when our politics contradict our faith, because we keep each thing in its own watertight compartment. But Chesterton was utterly consistent. He was consistent because his faith touched everything. He wrote about everything, and everything he wrote was imbued with his faith.

> You cannot evade the issue of God, whether you talk about pigs or the binomial theory, you are still talking about Him. Now if Christianity be ... a fragment of metaphysical nonsense invented by a few people, then, of course, defending it will simply mean talking that metaphysical nonsense over and over. But if Christianity should happen to be true—then defending it may mean talking about anything or everything. Things can be irrelevant to the proposition that Christianity is false, but nothing can be irrelevant to the proposition that Christianity is true.[25]

The fact that Chesterton wrote for a wide secular audience and always defended a Christian perspective is of course remarkable and unheard of in today's media. While it is one thing to say we should read Chesterton because he was important, it is even better to be able to say we *can* read Chesterton because he is still fresh and accessible. His newspaper articles are not just a historical curiosity. They are as pertinent today as when he wrote them three generations ago. And while some of his books have never gone out of print,

[25] *Daily News*, December 12, 1903.

many of them are back in print again because of a growing interest from those who have rediscovered this writer who is no longer taught in the schools.

But before you read Chesterton, be warned. He does not write like any other writer. You have to throw most of your expectations out the window and read him on his own terms. He will make you think. He will thrill you. He may frustrate you, and he may try your patience. There may be times when he seems to be floating airily, going nowhere or going everywhere at once, and then, like a hawk, he will suddenly swoop to a conclusion that will startle you. You will understand all at once that nothing he has said was irrelevant.

The most surprising thing about him is that there is nothing peculiar or bizarre or exotic about his ideas. You will find that all he does is express your own thoughts better than you are able to express them. You will find yourself saying, "But of course!" That is because he represents common sense. The only thing surprising about common sense is how uncommon it has become.

> The act of defending any of the cardinal virtues has today all the exhilaration of a vice.[26]

> Right is right, even if nobody does it. Wrong is wrong even if everybody is wrong about it.[27]

Chesterton claimed that he was doing nothing more than uttering plain, simple truths, but that they sounded so original and surprising and paradoxical because the world had come to expect something other than the truth. The world had things backwards. But he also said that sometimes truth

---

[26] *The Defendant* (New York: Dodd Mead, 1904), 97.
[27] *ILN*, May 11, 1907, *CW* 27:463.

has to come as a surprise, because that is the only way we will recognize and appreciate it.

More than one observer has described this three-hundred-pound, cigar-smoking journalist as a mystic. Well, Chesterton did say that there was a connection between mysticism and common sense. Both appeal to realities that we all know to be real even if we cannot prove them. He also said that mysticism is only a transcendent form of common sense. And that the ordinary man has always been a mystic.

Some have also called Chesterton a contemplative. Chesterton looked deeply into everything. He was always trying to find the universal. He certainly could not have defended the faith so well unless he had understood it intimately. And fortunately for us, since he wrote so much, we have the privilege of looking at his thoughts. We also have the advantage of having his vision enhance our own. Perhaps only a true contemplative could have said that if you look at a thing 999 times, you are perfectly safe, but if you look at it the thousandth time, you are in frightful danger of seeing it for the first time.[28]

The more you read Chesterton, the more you subject yourself to the frightful danger of seeing things for the first time.

[28] *The Napoleon of Notting Hill,* CW 6:227.

2

Orthodoxy

> People have fallen into a foolish habit of speaking of orthodoxy as something heavy, humdrum, and safe. There never was anything so perilous or so exciting as orthodoxy.
>
> — *Orthodoxy*

If you only read one book by Chesterton — well then shame on you—but if you only read one book by Chesterton, it has to be *Orthodoxy*.[1] It is possible that no one has ever defended the Christian faith with such wit and verve and vitality, with such surprising arguments and dazzling illustrations, as G. K. Chesterton does in *Orthodoxy*. This is the trunk of the tree from which all the other branches of Chesterton grow. It is a masterpiece of rhetoric; it has never been out of print since it was first published in 1908, and it is simply one of the best books written in the twentieth century.

Chesterton begins the book by describing a book he did not write, a "romance" about a man who sets sail from England in order to discover a new land. He accidentally gets

---

[1] However, if you read only *Orthodoxy*, you had better read it more than once.

turned around and returns to England, thinking it is the new place he had sought to discover, and finds himself looking at familiar things as if seeing them for the first time. Chesterton had intended to write that story as a way of illustrating what has to be one of life's greatest riddles and challenges:

> How can we contrive to be at once astonished at the world and yet at home in it?[2]

More importantly, Chesterton's unwritten story of romantic discovery is a metaphor for his own spiritual odyssey. He had set out to find a new and perfect religion. He knew all the things that it should include: wonder and mystery, beauty and artistry, freedom and obedience, gratitude and humility, dramatic sacrifice and gigantic joy. Just when he thought he had come up with this new religion, he was surprised to find that it already existed. It was Christianity.

> I have kept my truths: but I have discovered, not that they were not truths, but simply that they were not mine. When I fancied that I stood alone I was really in the ridiculous position of being backed up by all Christendom.... I did try to found a heresy of my own; and when I had put the last touches to it, I discovered that it was orthodoxy.[3]

When we read *Orthodoxy*, we have to be prepared to go on Chesterton's journey with him. It is full of surprising turns, and its destination is wonderful, but the first steps are the most important ones. It means the difference between getting home and getting lost.

The first step is to accept the reality of sin, which should not be that hard to do.

---

[2] *Orthodoxy, CW* 1:212.
[3] Ibid., 214.

Certain new theologians dispute original sin, which is the only part of Christian theology which can really be proved. . . . They . . . deny human sin, which they can see in the street. The strongest saints and the strongest sceptics alike took positive evil as the starting-point of their argument. If it be true (as it certainly is) that a man can feel exquisite happiness in skinning a cat, then the religious philosopher can only draw one of two deductions. He must either deny the existence of God, as all atheists do; or he must deny the present union between God and man, as all Christians do. The new theologians seem to think it a highly rationalistic solution to deny the cat.[4]

The next step is to accept the limits of reason. Chesterton, in all his writings, never attacks reason but always defends it and is always reasonable in his arguments. However, the point here is that reason can take us only so far and that those who rely solely on reason are setting a trap for themselves. Reason must be supplemented by our creative imagination and by faith.

The madman is not the man who has lost his reason. The madman is the man who has lost everything except his reason.[5]

Poets do not go mad; but chess-players do. Mathematicians go mad, and cashiers; but creative artists very seldom.[6]

Poetry is sane because it floats easily in an infinite sea; reason seeks to cross the infinite sea, and so make it finite. . . . The poet only asks to get his head into the heavens. It is the

[4] Ibid., 217.
[5] Ibid., 222.
[6] Ibid., 219.

logician who seeks to get the heavens into his head. And it is his head that splits.[7]

Chesterton says that reason is itself an act of faith.

It is an act of faith to assert that our thoughts have any relation to reality at all.[8]

The real trouble with this world of ours is not that it is an unreasonable world, nor even that it is a reasonable one. The commonest kind of trouble is that it is nearly reasonable, but not quite. Life is not an illogicality; yet it is a trap for logicians. It looks just a little more mathematical and regular than it is; its exactitude is obvious, but its inexactitude is hidden.[9]

So if reliance on reason alone is a recipe for insanity, what is the solution to the riddle? The answer lies in the concept of paradox, which is not only the key to *Orthodoxy*, it is one of most important themes throughout all of Chesterton's writings. There is a contradiction at the heart of all things. It is a contradiction that philosophers and logicians cannot explain away. It is a mystery. It is a knot that cannot be untied. But while the modern intellectual may choke on the paradox, it is the daily bread of the common man. Because the common man has something that the modern intellectual is sadly lacking: common sense.

The ordinary man has always been sane because the ordinary man has always been a mystic. He has permitted the twilight. He has always had one foot in earth and the other in fairyland. He has always left himself free to doubt his gods;

[7] Ibid., 220.
[8] Ibid., 236.
[9] Ibid., 285.

but (unlike the agnostic of to-day) free also to believe in them. He has always cared more for truth than for consistency. If he saw two truths that seemed to contradict each other, he would take the two truths and the contradiction along with them. His spiritual sight is stereoscopic, like his physical sight: he sees two different pictures at once and yet sees all the better for that. Thus he has always believed that there was such a thing as fate, but such a thing as free will also. Thus he believed that children were indeed the kingdom of heaven, but nevertheless ought to be obedient to the kingdom of earth.... It is exactly this balance of apparent contradictions that has been the whole buoyancy of the healthy man. The whole secret of mysticism is this: that man can understand everything by the help of what he does not understand. The morbid logician seeks to make everything lucid, and succeeds in making everything mysterious. The mystic allows one thing to be mysterious, and everything else becomes lucid. The determinist makes the theory of causation quite clear, and then finds that he cannot say "if you please" to the housemaid. The Christian permits free will to remain a sacred mystery; but because of this his relations with the housemaid become of a sparkling and crystal clearness.... As ... the circle [is] the symbol of reason and madness ... the cross [is] the symbol ... of mystery and of health.... For the circle is perfect and infinite in its nature; but it is fixed forever in its size; it can never be larger or smaller. But the cross, though it has at its heart a collision and a contradiction, can extend its four arms for ever without altering its shape. Because it has a paradox in its centre it can grow without changing. The circle returns upon itself and is bound. The cross opens its arms to the four winds; it is a signpost for free travellers.[10]

[10] Ibid., 230–31.

Chesterton's rejection of determinism or fatalism, whether it be scientific or Calvinistic, is very important. Free will is one of the most sacred truths of Catholic theology, because it affirms our dignity as human beings and makes both our confession and our praise worthwhile. If there is no free will, well, then there is no reason to discuss it. A man who does not believe in free will cannot even say Please pass the mustard.

Freedom is glorious, but freedom is enjoyed only within the rules. We are defined by our limits, like the frame around a picture. You can free a tiger from his bars, but you cannot free him from his stripes.

Freedom gives us the privilege to govern ourselves, which is the essence, of course, of democracy. And Chesterton is a great believer in democracy.

He says there may be some things that we do not want a man to do unless he does them well: discover the North Pole, play the church organ, write poetry. But the exercise of democracy is not one of those things. Democracy means writing your own love letters and blowing your own nose. Democracy means "that the most terribly important things must be left to ordinary men themselves—the mating of the sexes, the rearing of the young", and the making of laws.[11]

Now, Chesterton extends this defense of democracy in a surprising direction: into the past. He connects democracy with tradition.

> Tradition means giving votes to the most obscure of all classes, our ancestors. It is the democracy of the dead.[12]

One of the voices—or votes—of tradition is the fairy tale, the stories told and retold across generations, not because

[11] Ibid., 250.
[12] Ibid., 251.

they never happened, but because they always happen. They are the stories of normal people in abnormal situations, tests of love and valor, maidens who need to be rescued and dragons that need to be slain. Chesterton called these things "The Ethics of Elfland". And there are five particular lessons he learned in Elfland that led to his surprising discovery of the Christian faith:

First, the world does not explain itself. We need someone or something else to explain it to us. Secondly, the magic and wonder in the world must mean something, and if it means something, there must be someone to mean it. Thirdly, the created world is beautiful in its design (even if there are exceptions, like dragons). Fourthly, this creation comes to us as a gift, something we do not deserve. Thus we have a debt of gratitude. And gratitude is best expressed by humility and restraint: "we should thank God for beer and Burgundy by not drinking too much of them." And fifthly, there is a sense that we have been saved from a primordial ruin, as Robinson Crusoe was saved from a shipwreck.[13]

Now, when Chesterton went on to examine the Christian faith he found that it confirmed the truths he had already discovered. He also discovered that Christianity was rational even if it was not simple. It was complicated, but that, too, was one of its glories. It was sometimes odd, but, as he says,

> Whenever we feel there is something odd in Christian theology, we shall generally find that there is something odd in the truth.[14]

---

[13] Ibid., 268.
[14] Ibid., 286.

The truth of Christianity extended across history and places and people. He found it to be, indeed, universal.

> An imbecile habit has arisen in modern controversy of saying that such and such a creed can be held in one age but cannot be held in another. Some dogma, we are told, was credible in the twelfth century, but is not credible in the twentieth. You might as well say that a certain philosophy can be believed on Mondays, but cannot be believed on Tuesdays.... What a man can believe depends upon his philosophy, not upon the clock or the century. If a man believes in unalterable natural law, he cannot believe in any miracle in any age. If a man believes in a will behind law, he can believe in any miracle in any age.[15]

Anything can be believed in any age. But, oddly enough, there really is a sense in which a creed, if it is believed at all, can be believed more fixedly in a complex society than in a simple one.

> If [a creed] is right at all, it is a compliment to say that it's elaborately right. A stick might fit a hole or a stone a hollow by accident. But a key and a lock are both complex. And if a key fits a lock, you know it is the right key.
>
> But this involved accuracy of the thing makes it very difficult to do what I now have to do, to describe this accumulation of truth. It is very hard for a man to defend anything of which he is entirely convinced. It is comparatively easy when he is only partially convinced. He is partially convinced because he has found this or that proof of the thing, and he can expound it. But a man is not really convinced of a philosophic theory when he finds that something proves it.

[15] Ibid., 278.

He is only really convinced when he finds that everything proves it.[16]

So, in the end, Chesterton accepted the Christian religion, in all its fullness and complexity and completeness, rather than settling for the scattered and simplistic and secular truths outside of it. He discovered that not only is the faith the mother of all worldly energies, but its foes are the fathers of all worldly confusion. He says:

> The secularists have not wrecked divine things; but the secularists have wrecked secular things, if that is any comfort to them.[17]

He discovered that paradox is the key to truth, and that the ultimate paradox is the key to ultimate truth. And the ultimate paradox is Jesus Christ: fully God and fully man. Not half God and half man, like a centaur. Not a creature neither God nor man, like an elf, but both things at once, in all their fullness.

Chesterton discovered another paradox: that the key to happiness is humility. And he expresses the essence of humility perhaps better than any writer ever has:

> Angels fly because they take themselves lightly.[18]

Chesterton saw almost a century ago that liberalizing theologians do not liberate. Changing the theology, changing the rules, does not bring freedom. Only truth brings freedom.

---

[16] Ibid., 287.

[17] Ibid., 345.

[18] Chesterton's most famous line. And it is always misquoted. In fact, we misquoted it, too. It is actually: "Angels can fly because they can take themselves lightly", ibid., 325.

And truth does not change. Chesterton makes the extraordinary observation:

> Catholic doctrine and discipline may be walls; but they are
> the walls of a playground.[19]

If we take away the walls of doctrine and discipline, we take away not only the means of keeping the faith safe and secure, but the means of keeping the faith fun, of protecting the joy that is inside. And there is great joy inside.

> The unpopular parts of Christianity turn out when examined to be the very props of the people. The outer ring of Christianity is a rigid guard of ethical abnegations and professional priests; but inside that inhuman guard you will find the old human life dancing like children, and drinking wine like men; for Christianity is the only frame for pagan freedom. But in the modern philosophy the case is opposite; it is its outer ring that is obviously artistic and emancipated; its despair is within.[20]

> Joy, which was the small publicity of the pagan, is the gigantic secret of the Christian.... The tremendous figure which fills the Gospels towers in this respect, as in every other, above all the thinkers who ever thought themselves tall. His pathos was natural, almost casual. The Stoics, ancient and modern, were proud of concealing their tears. He never concealed His tears; He showed them plainly on His open face at any daily sight, such as the far sight of His native city. Yet He concealed something. Solemn supermen and imperial diplomatists are proud of restraining their anger. He never restrained His anger. He flung furniture down the front steps of the Temple, and asked men how they expected to

escape the damnation of Hell. Yet He restrained something. I say it with reverence; there was in that shattering personality a thread that must be called shyness. There was something that He hid from all men when He went up a mountain to pray. There was something that He covered constantly by abrupt silence or impetuous isolation. There was some one thing that was too great for God to show us when He walked upon our earth; and I have sometimes fancied that it was His mirth.[21]

Chesterton's journey to orthodoxy was a remarkable one. It was the thrill of discovering the truth, and then the surprise of discovering that he was not the first to discover it. His fascinating account of the journey is one of the most original and brightest defenses of the Christian faith ever written. But what is perhaps even more remarkable is that it is also such a powerful defense of the Catholic faith. Why is that so remarkable? Because *Orthodoxy* was written fourteen years before Chesterton became a Catholic.

[21] Ibid., 365–66.

3

Heretics

The human brain is a machine for coming to conclusions; if it cannot come to conclusions it is rusty. When we hear of a man too clever to believe,... it is like hearing of a nail that was too good to hold down a carpet; or a bolt that was too strong to keep a door shut.... Man can be defined as an animal that makes dogmas. As he piles doctrine on doctrine and conclusion on conclusion in the formation of some ... philosophy or religion, he is ... becoming more and more human. When he drops one doctrine after another in a refined scepticism, when he declines to tie himself to a system, when he says that he has outgrown definitions,... holding no form of creed but contemplating all, then he is by that very process sinking slowly backwards into the vagueness of the vagrant animals and the unconsciousness of the grass. Trees have no dogmas. Turnips are singularly broad-minded.

—Heretics

If you are a turnip, you may not be interested in reading G. K. Chesterton. But if you have a brain, and like the idea of using it to come to conclusions, Chesterton is just right for you.

Heretics is one of Chesterton's most important books. It is also, for some reason, one of his most neglected books. Perhaps the reason has to do with the title. The word "heretic" conjures up frightful images of controversial characters being barbecued for their beliefs. It smacks of "intolerance". The very word "dogmatic" is perceived as being intolerant. As Chesterton says, however, man is the animal who makes dogmas. You could say that man is a religious animal. There is something ironic about the ideal of "tolerance" or so-called religious freedom. It has done more to suppress religion than has any persecution. It has left us not only afraid to debate our beliefs, it has made us afraid even to discuss them. As Chesterton says we now talk about "the weather, and call it the complete liberty of all creeds." [1] This strange silence about religion leaves the impression that religion is not important.

> There is one thing that is infinitely more absurd and unprac-
> tical than burning a man for his philosophy. This is the habit
> of saying that his philosophy does not matter, and this is done
> universally in the twentieth century.... A man's opinion ...
> on Botticelli matters; his opinion on all things does not
> matter. [2]

Chesterton says that we cannot get away from the fact that we have a general view of existence, whether we like it or not, and that it affects and involves everything we say or do, whether we like it or not. And our general view of things is based on our ultimate view of things. Religion is never irrelevant. It deals not only with ultimate things but with everything else.

[1] *Heretics, CW* 1:41.
[2] Ibid., 40.

It is important to note that Chesterton's book is not an attack but a defense. A defense of the ancient truths that are under attack by modern heretics. Chesterton claims to have gained a deeper appreciation of the Christian faith through the simple exercise of defending it.

> We who are Christians never knew the great philosophic common sense which inheres in that mystery until the anti-Christian writers pointed it out to us.[3]

Common sense. The Christian faith is common sense. Heresy, it turns out, is usually a distinct lack of common sense.

A heresy is at best a half-truth, but usually even less than that. A heresy is a fragment of the truth that is exaggerated at the expense of the rest of the truth. For instance, freedom is good, but that does not mean obedience is bad. Sobriety is good, but that does not mean wine is bad. Sacrifice is good, but that does not mean pleasure is bad. Reason is good, but that does not mean faith is bad. In the Catholic faith, we recognize that a heresy is not so much a false doctrine as an incomplete doctrine. It has rejected part of the truth and is representing what is left over as the whole truth. But what the heretic usually ends up doing is attacking the greater truth. The reason why Chesterton is an apostle of common sense is that he is a complete thinker. The reason he could recognize heresy is because he could expose incomplete thinking.

Surprisingly, Chesterton wrote *Heretics* before he became a Catholic. Although he defends the Christian faith generally, he is already defending Catholic doctrine specifically. The completeness of his thought is already apparent. For

---

[3] Ibid., 206.

instance, he gives a very Catholic response to the heresy that strong societies can only be established by strong men:

> When Christ at a symbolic moment was establishing His great society, He chose for its corner-stone neither the brilliant Paul nor the mystic John, but a shuffler, a snob, a coward—in a word, a man. And upon this rock He has built His Church, and the gates of Hell have not prevailed against it. All the empires and the kingdoms have failed, because of this inherent and continual weakness, that they were founded by strong men and upon strong men. But this one thing, the historic Christian Church, was founded on a weak man, and for that reason it is indestructible. For no chain is stronger than its weakest link.[4]

The so-called heretics that Chesterton writes about in this book were his philosophical and political opponents, people like George Bernard Shaw and H. G. Wells. Chesterton treats them with fairness and with geniality. He points out what is good in their argument before pointing out what is fatally wrong. His geniality is as great as his genius, but we should not underestimate his courage and his confidence. He is, after all, going up against the leading thinkers of the day and telling them that they are wrong and why they are wrong. The list of personalities includes Shaw and Wells and other well-known names, along with some names that are probably no longer familiar. But all the heresies are familiar. Especially to the modern world, which praises science and hygiene and success and progress. These are all very well and good, but they have been elevated at the expense of larger truths, such as faith and tradition and humility and lasting ideals.

[4] Ibid., 70.

These larger truths lie at the heart of Christianity. Chesterton says that Christianity better understands man's needs than any modern philosophy or economic system or political scheme or social policy. Christianity may be an ideal, but the Christian mystic, says Chesterton, is the most practical man of all. He does the right thing and for the right reason. The heretic may occasionally do the right thing for the wrong reason. But doing things for the right reason, says Chesterton, "is always jollier".[5]

> A young man may keep himself from vice by continually thinking of disease. He may keep himself from it also by continually thinking of the Virgin Mary. There may be question about which method is the more reasonable, or even about which is the more efficient. But surely there can be no question about which is the more wholesome.[6]

Chesterton is usually able to use the heretics' own arguments against them. As he says, it was the anti-Christian writers who pointed out all the common sense in Christianity. In the same way it is often the agnostics and scoffers who provide some of the best evidence for the very existence of God. For example, says Chesterton, blasphemy is based on belief. The blasphemer cannot achieve any artistic effect unless he is at heart a believer. "If anyone doubts this," says Chesterton, "let him sit down seriously and try to think blasphemous thoughts about Thor."[7]

Likewise he shows how the skepticism of the skeptic is his own undoing. The agnostic who cannot make up his mind about anything will still maintain that he can see the good in

[5] Ibid., 48.
[6] Ibid.
[7] Ibid., 44.

everything because of his open-mindedness. Chesterton says it is ludicrous to suppose that the more skeptical we are, the more we see good in everything. Rather, the more we are certain what good is, the more we shall see good in everything. We have to have some conviction of the truth in order to see the good. But it cannot be an idiosyncratic truth. It has to be a shared truth. In other words, it has to be common sense. It is no great praise to say of some eccentric intellectual, "He knows his own mind." Chesterton says that is like saying, "He blows his own nose." [8]

Let us take a look at how Chesterton deals with a few of the modern heresies. First up: progress. How can anybody be against progress? Well, the problem with progress, Chesterton points out, is that it does not mean anything.

You cannot have progress unless you have established what your goal is. Progress itself cannot be a goal. Progress cannot be an ideal. Chesterton says, the word "is simply a comparative of which we have not settled the superlative." [9]

> Nobody has any business to use the word "progress" unless he has a definite creed and a cast-iron code of morals. Nobody can be progressive without being doctrinal.... For progress by its very name indicates a direction; and the moment we are in the least doubtful about the direction, we become in the same degree doubtful about the progress. Never perhaps since the beginning of the world has there been an age that had less right to use the word "progress" than we. In the Catholic twelfth century, in the philosophic eighteenth century, the direction may have been a good or a bad one, men may have differed more or less about how far they went, and in what direction, but about the direction they did in

[8] Ibid., 203.
[9] Ibid., 52.

the main agree, and consequently they had the genuine sensation of progress. But it is precisely about the direction that we disagree. Whether the future excellence lies in more law or less law, in more liberty or less liberty; whether property will be finally concentrated or finally cut up; whether sexual passion will reach its sanest in an almost virgin intellectualism or in a full animal freedom; whether we should love everybody with Tolstoy, or spare nobody with Nietzsche;—these are the things about which we are actually fighting most.[10]

Next, science. What is wrong with science? Nothing. Science is good, as far as it can go. But there are some places where science cannot go. It cannot go into the soul. It cannot explain human nature. If someone does try to use science to explain human nature, that is a misuse of science. It is vain to try to explain the soul in materialistic terms. It is also dangerous. To deny the reality of the spiritual world has far-reaching ramifications in the material world. As Chesterton says:

> Take away the supernatural, and what remains is the unnatural.[11]

Chesterton criticizes the very idea that if we scientifically study primitive cultures, we can then understand our own culture, that if we examine tribal beliefs, we can then scientifically uncover the basis for our religion.

> If a man desires to find out the origins of religions, let him not go to the Sandwich Islands; let him go to church.... We do not understand the savage for the same reason that the savage does not understand himself. And the savage does not

[10] Ibid., 53.
[11] Ibid., 88.

understand himself for the same reason that we do not understand ourselves either.

The obvious truth is that the moment any matter has passed through the human mind it ... has become a thing incurably mysterious and infinite.... Even what we call our material desires are spiritual, because they are human. Science can analyse a pork-chop, and say how much of it is phosphorus and how much is protein; but science cannot analyse any man's wish for a pork-chop, and say how much of it is hunger, how much custom, how much nervous fancy, how much a haunting love of the beautiful. The man's desire for the pork-chop remains literally as mystical and ethereal as his desire for heaven. All attempts, therefore, at a science of any human things, at a science of history, a science of folk-lore, a science of sociology, are by their nature not merely hopeless, but crazy.[12]

Next up, paganism. Modern heretics think themselves quite clever in saying that paganism is superior to Christianity, and they even imagine themselves able to be pagans. Chesterton shows that not only was paganism something different from what the moderns think it was, it was something much less than the Christianity that replaced it. Modern intellectuals, by pretending to be pagans, only show how narrow they are.

The real difference between Paganism and Christianity is perfectly summed up in the difference between the pagan, or natural, virtues, and those three virtues of Christianity which the Church of Rome calls virtues of grace ... faith, hope, and charity.... The pagan virtues, such as justice and temperance, are the sad virtues, and ... the mystical virtues of faith, hope, and charity are the gay and exuberant vir-

tues.... The pagan virtues are the reasonable virtues, and ...
the Christian virtues of faith, hope, and charity are ... unreasonable.... Justice consists in finding out a certain thing
due to a certain man and giving it to him. Temperance consists in finding out the proper limit of a particular indul-
gence and adhering to that. But charity means pardoning
what is unpardonable, or it is no virtue at all. Hope means
hoping when things are hopeless, or it is no virtue at all.
And faith means believing the incredible, or it is no virtue at
all.[13]

As we said earlier, *Heretics* is a book that defends good things
much more than it attacks bad things. And there is one chapter in the book that is truly marvelous. In fact, one observer[14] has said it is the quintessential Chesterton essay, that if
we could keep only one piece of his writing and everything
else that Chesterton ever wrote were to be burned or bur-
ied, this is the chapter we should keep. The chapter is called
"On Certain Modern Writers and the Institution of the Family". Chesterton understands the importance and centrality
of the family in society. He calls the family the ultimate human institution. Obviously if the family is under attack, so is
the whole society. But there is another surprising lesson here,
filled with an even greater common sense. It is this: If we can
get along in a family, we can get along in other lesser human
institutions, like neighborhoods or cities or countries.

It is a good thing for a man to live in a family for the same reason that it is a good thing for a man to be besieged in a city. It
is a good thing for a man to live in a family in the same sense
that it is a beautiful and delightful thing for a man to be snowed

[13] Ibid., 124–25.
[14] John Peterson, in a symposium on *Heretics* at the Midwest Chesterton
Conference, Milwaukee, Wisconsin, June 1994.

up in a street. They all force him to realize that life is not a thing from outside, but a thing from inside.... Life, if it be a truly stimulating and fascinating life, is a thing which, of its nature, exists in spite of ourselves. The modern writers who have suggested ... that the family is a bad institution, have generally confined themselves to suggesting, with much sharpness, bitterness, or pathos, that perhaps the family is not always very congenial. Of course the family is a good institution because it is uncongenial. It is wholesome precisely because it contains so many divergencies and varieties. It is, as the sentimentalists say, like a little kingdom, and, like most other little kingdoms, is generally in a state of something resembling anarchy.... The men and women who, for good reasons and bad, revolt against the family, are, for good reasons and bad, simply revolting against mankind. Aunt Elizabeth is unreasonable, like mankind. Papa is excitable, like mankind. Our youngest brother is mischievous, like mankind. Grandpapa is stupid, like the world; he is old, like the world.

Those who wish, rightly or wrongly, to step out of all this, do definitely wish to step into a narrower world. They are dismayed and terrified by the largeness and variety of the family.... I do not say, for a moment, that the flight to this narrower life may not be the right thing for the individual, any more than I say the same thing about flight into a monastery. But I do say that anything is bad and artificial which tends to make these people succumb to the strange delusion that they are stepping into a world which is actually larger and more varied than their own. The best way that a man could test his readiness to encounter the common variety of mankind would be to climb down a chimney into any house at random, and get on as well as possible with the people inside. And that is essentially what each one of us did on the day that he was born.[15]

[15] *Heretics, CW* 1:141–42.

Chesterton says, The supreme adventure is being born. When we step into the world, it is like stepping into a splendid and startling trap. It is something we do not expect. When we step into a family we step into a fairy tale. It is romantic, fantastic, colorful, and sometimes hardly believable. Like a fairy tale, it is a story. If there is a story, there is a storyteller. Each day is a new chapter. And, says Chesterton, in the fiery alphabet of every sunset is written, "to be continued in our next".[16]

[16] Ibid., 143.

4

What's Wrong with the World

There was a time when you and I and all of us were all
very close to God; so that even now the color of a pebble
..., the smell of a flower ..., comes to our hearts with a
kind of authority and certainty; as if they were fragments
of a muddled message, or features of a forgotten face. To
pour that fiery simplicity upon the whole of life is the
only real aim of education; and closest to the child comes
the woman—she understands.... [S]he understands ...
[the] uproarious amateurishness of the universe, such as
we felt when we were little.... She was juggling with
frantic and flaming suns.... She was maintaining the prime
truth of woman, the universal mother: that if a thing is
worth doing, it is worth doing badly.

—*What's Wrong with the World*

A thing worth doing is worth doing ... *badly?* G. K. Chesterton will always surprise you.

Chesterton's book *What's Wrong with the World* was written in 1910. However, reading it now, you might be tempted
to think it had been written today. The book is probably
more timely now than when he wrote it.

Our society is experiencing exactly the crisis that Chesterton warned us about almost a century ago. There is a greater

44

disparity than ever between the rich and poor. Our families are falling apart; our schools are in utter chaos; our basic freedoms are under assault. The crisis affects every one of us. As Chesterton says:

Not only are we all in the same boat, but we are all seasick.[1]

But, he says, while we agree about the evil, we no longer agree about the good.

I have called this book "What Is Wrong with the World?" and the upshot of the title can be easily and clearly stated. What is wrong is that we do not ask what is right.[2]

Some people say that idealism is impractical. Chesterton, however, says:

Idealism is only considering everything in its practical essence.[3]

In other words, idealism is common sense. It is what the common man knows is right, in spite of all the voices telling him it is impractical or unrealistic or outdated. And when Chesterton says idealism, he means the Christian ideal.

The Christian ideal has not been tried and found wanting. It has been found difficult; and left untried.[4]

The Christian ideal would create the best kind of society and would correct the ills suffered by today's society. Chesterton says it must be a society based on the ideal house, the happy family, the holy family of history. It means making laws that respect the family as the most important unit of

---

[1] *What's Wrong with the World, CW* 4:95.
[2] Ibid., 41.
[3] Ibid., 43.
[4] Ibid., 61.

society and laws that are moral and respect religious principles. It means the widespread distribution of property and capital to provide for greater justice and liberty. It means not being afraid to teach the truth to our children. But we have left the truth behind us. And instead of turning around and going back and fixing things, we rush madly forward toward we know not what and call ourselves "progressive". It is time to defend the family and the Church and the republic. Chesterton says these things are now assailed by those who have never known them or by those who have failed to fulfill them.

> Men invent new ideals because they dare not attempt old ideals. They look forward with enthusiasm, because they are afraid to look back[5]

> There is one metaphor of which the moderns are very fond; they are always saying, "You can't put the clock back." The simple and obvious answer is "You can." A clock, being a piece of human construction, can be restored by the human finger to any figure or hour. In the same way society, being a piece of human construction, can be reconstructed upon any plan that has ever existed.
> There is another proverb, "As you have made your bed, so you must lie on it"; which again is simply a lie. If I have made my bed uncomfortable, please God I will make it again.[6]

Although this book is nonfiction, Chesterton introduces us to two characters: Hudge and Gudge. Well, three characters: he also introduces us to Jones. Hudge and Gudge are the enemies of Jones. Hudge is the "energetic progressive", a socialist. Gudge is the "obstinate conservative", an

[5] Ibid., 54.
[6] Ibid., 57.

industrialist-capitalist. In other words, Hudge is Big Government, and Gudge is Big Business.

And Jones? Jones is the common man. This man Jones, says Chesterton, has always desired "ordinary things; he has married for love, he has chosen or built a small house that fits like a coat; he is ready to be a great grandfather" and a local hero.[7] But something has gone wrong. Hudge and Gudge have conspired against Jones to take away his property, his independence, and his dignity.

Chesterton says that "the home is the only place of liberty."[8]

Property is merely the art of democracy.[9]

It means that every man should have something that he can shape in his own image. To give nearly everybody ordinary houses would please nearly everybody. In a society where most people cannot afford their own home; when they cannot properly support themselves, but have to be someone else's wage slave, easily sacked, easily replaced and displaced, having to rely on the government to supplement their needs; in other words, when they are totally at the mercy of Hudge and Gudge, it means enormous pressure is put on the family, and it means the society will crumble from the bottom up. The society is especially in danger when the common man, left reeling by the loss of religion, of home, of family, is not even sure what he wants any more.

Man has always lost his way. He has been a tramp ever since Eden; but he always knew, or thought he knew, what he was

[7] Ibid., 82.
[8] Ibid., 72.
[9] Ibid., 66.

looking for. Every man has a house somewhere in the elaborate cosmos; his house waits for him.... But in the bleak and blinding hail of skepticism to which he has been now so long subjected, he has begun for the first time to be chilled, not merely in his hopes, but in his desires. For the first time in history he begins really to doubt the object of his wanderings on earth. He has always lost his way; but now he has lost his address.[10]

Chesterton says that neither industrialism nor collectivism is an ideal, but they have been accepted as necessities. We do not have to give in to Hudge and Gudge. To do so, he says, is "the huge modern heresy of altering the human soul to fit its conditions, instead of altering human conditions to fit the human soul".[11]

It may surprise us to realize that specialization is the enemy of democracy. It is also the enemy of religion, as one by one each of the functions of religion is taken over by narrow secular interests.

Religion, the immortal maiden, has been a maid-of-all-work as well as a servant of mankind. She provided men at once with the theoretic laws of an unalterable cosmos; and also with the practical rules of the rapid and thrilling game of morality. She taught logic to the student and told fairy tales to the children; it was her business to confront the nameless gods whose fears are on all flesh, and also to see ... that there was a day for wearing ribbons or an hour for ringing bells. The large uses of religion have been broken up into lesser specialties.... The romance of ritual and colored emblem has been taken over by that narrowest of all trades, modern art (the sort called art for art's sake), and men are in modern practice informed that they may use all symbols so long as they mean nothing by them. The romance of conscience has been dried up into the science of ethics; which may well be called decency for decency's sake.... Everything has been sundered from everything else, and everything has grown cold. Soon we shall hear of specialists dividing the tune from the words of a song, on the ground that they spoil each other; and I did once meet a man who openly advocated the separation of almonds and raisins. This world is all one wild divorce court.[12]

Traditionally, there has been one key person in society who has prevented the total degeneration into specialization, into this separating of everything from everything else. That person is the woman.

Chesterton's view of women may be difficult for some people to understand. Because some people cannot understand simple, basic ideas. He does not think men and women are equal. He thinks women are superior to men. He thinks that for women to seek equality would be a step downward. Also, when he says that men and women are not equal, he means—this may be shocking—that they are not the same.

Chesterton says women are more dignified than men and more practical than men. And, women are broad, whereas men are narrow.

Women were not kept at home in order to keep them narrow; on the contrary, they were kept at home in order to keep them broad. The world outside the home was one mass of narrowness, a maze of cramped paths, a madhouse of monomaniacs.[13]

It is not difficult to see why ... the female became the emblem of the universal.... Nature ... surrounded her with very young children, who require to be taught not so much anything as everything. Babies need not to be taught a trade, but to be introduced to a world. To put the matter shortly, woman is generally shut up in a house with a human being at the time when he asks all the questions that there are, and some that there aren't. It would be odd if she retained any of the narrowness of a specialist. Now if anyone says that this duty of general enlightenment ... is in itself too exacting and oppressive, I can understand the view. I can only answer that our race has thought it worth while to cast this burden on women in order to keep common-sense in the world. But when people begin to talk about this domestic duty as not merely difficult but trivial and dreary, I simply give up the question. For I cannot with the utmost energy of imagination conceive what they mean. When domesticity, for instance, is called drudgery, all the difficulty arises from a double meaning in the word. If drudgery only means dreadfully hard work, I admit the woman drudges in the home, as a man might drudge at the Cathedral of Amiens or drudge behind a gun at Trafalgar. But if it means that the hard work is more heavy because it is trifling, colorless and of small import to the soul, then as I say, I give it up; I do not know what the words mean.... How can it be a large career to tell other people's children about the Rule of Three, and a small career to tell one's own children about the universe? How can it be broad to be the same thing to everyone, and narrow to be everything to someone? No; a woman's function is labo-

[13] Ibid., 116.

rious, but because it is gigantic, not because it is minute. I will pity Mrs. Jones for the hugeness of her task; I will never pity her for its smallness.[14]

It is common sense, though for some reason we need Chesterton to point it out to us, that if you take the mother out of the family, you destroy the family.

Remember Hudge and Gudge? They are together in this conspiracy against the family. Hudge claims to be "freeing" the woman from the home. Gudge is happy to have her out of the home because he depends on her as a source of cheap labor.

> Most of the Feminists would probably agree with me that womanhood is under shameful tyranny in the shops and mills. But I want to destroy tyranny. They want to destroy womanhood. That is the only difference.[15]

Feminists have never realized what unwitting players they have been in the scheme of Hudge and Gudge. Chesterton once said, "Ten million young women rose to their feet with the cry, *We will not be dictated to*: and proceeded to become stenographers." [16]

Chesterton quite frankly does not want women to become involved in government—not because he does not want women to have more power, but because he does not want government to have more power. Women already have the supreme power in society, because they are the natural rulers of the household. Men run off and make governments,

[14] Ibid., 117–19.
[15] Ibid., 149.
[16] Maisie Ward, *Gilbert Keith Chesterton* (New York: Sheed and Ward, 1942), 205.

which are never quite as important as men claim they are. Most women figured this out. The feminists did not. They bought into men's claims about the importance of politics, and, with Hudge's help, government has grown to ridiculous proportions and has threatened the authority and primacy of the family, as it insinuates itself into every aspect of our lives.

The next thing that is wrong with the world is education. Chesterton explains exactly why our schools have failed. "Education", he says, "is only truth in a state of transmission." [17] If we do not agree on the truth, how can we teach it to our children?

Remember, this was in 1910; yet already Chesterton recognizes the subtle tendency toward new educational theories—such as the idea that education is not instruction at all, that the teacher is simply there to "draw out" of the child his own inherent knowledge and abilities.

> You may indeed "draw out" squeals and grunts from the child by simply poking him and pulling him about, a pleasant but cruel pastime to which many psychologists are addicted. But you will wait and watch very patiently indeed before you draw the English language out of him. That you have got to put into him; and there is an end of the matter. [18]

> [We are] shrinking from ... the responsibility of affirming the truth of our human tradition and handing it on with a voice of authority, an unshaken voice. That is the one eternal education; to be sure enough that something is true that you dare to tell it to a child. From this high audacious duty the moderns are fleeing on every side; and the only excuse

[17] *What's Wrong with the World, CW* 4:164.
[18] Ibid., 165.

for them is (of course,) that their modern philosophies are so half-baked and hypothetical that they cannot convince themselves enough to convince even a newborn babe.... Obviously, it ought to be the oldest things that are taught to the youngest people; the assured and experienced truths that are put first to the baby. But in a school to-day the baby has to submit to a system that is younger than himself.[19]

Chesterton says:

There are no uneducated people. Everybody ... is educated; only most people are educated wrong.[20]

He points out that we are no longer teaching history, but hygiene; we are no longer teaching traditional ideals, but the fashionable ideals of the governing class—Hudge and Gudge. And not only are we creating nothing but specialists rather than well-rounded individuals, but we have come to rely solely on specialists to be the teachers, the counselors, the technicians. Chesterton says:

The only persons who seem to have nothing to do with the education of the children are the parents.[21]

What's wrong with the world? There is a crisis that begins in the home and reaches to the workplace and the classroom. We need a solution, and we need the right solution. The situation is desperate, and desperately calls on us to find the right solution. Chesterton says:

[19] Ibid., 167.
[20] Ibid., 171.
[21] Ibid., 194.

> It is wrong to fiddle while Rome is burning; but it is quite right to study the theory of hydraulics while Rome is burning.[22]

Chesterton's solution is that we have to repent and return to the Christian ideal. The only step forward is a step back. We know what we have to do, and Chesterton says,

> There is only one really startling thing to be done with the ideal, and that is to do it.[23]

[22] Ibid., 43.
[23] Ibid., 64.

5

The Catholic Church and Conversion

Becoming a Catholic broadens the mind. It especially
broadens the mind about the reasons for becoming a Catholic. Standing in the centre where all roads meet, a man
can look down each of the roads in turn and realise that
they come from all points of the heavens.

— *The Catholic Church and Conversion*

When G. K. Chesterton was asked why he became a Catholic, his short answer was: "To get rid of my sins." [1] For the
longer answer, he wrote a book. And that book was *The
Catholic Church and Conversion*.

Chesterton was received into the Catholic Church in 1922,
at the age of forty-eight, after what was a very long and
steady and deliberate conversion. Though he had already written eloquently and forcefully in defense of the Catholic faith,
and though he had even written a famous book of mystery
stories featuring an amateur detective who was a Roman Catholic priest, Chesterton waited a long time before becoming
a Catholic himself.

---

[1] *Autobiography, CW* 16:319.

He tells part of his story in *The Catholic Church and Conversion*, which he wrote in 1927, five years after he joined the Church. But before we examine that book, there are two things that should be mentioned about that day in 1922 when G. K. Chesterton was received into the Catholic Church.

First of all, that famous detective, Father Brown, was based on a real priest who had become a close friend of Chesterton. His name was Father John O'Connor. When Chesterton informed Father O'Connor of his decision, the priest gave him a copy of the *Penny Catechism* to read. And on the morning he was to be received into the Church, Chesterton was seen reading it. Afterward he said that when he read it, he was struck by an expression that seemed exactly to sum up something he had been trying to express all his life. It was the statement, "The two sins against hope are presumption and despair." [2] He said that the heresies that have attacked human happiness in his time, were all variations either of presumption or of despair.

And after receiving his First Communion that Sunday morning, Chesterton wrote a poem called "The Convert", which is probably his most personal statement about his conversion:

> After one moment when I bowed my head
> And the whole world turned over and came upright,
> And I came out where the old road shone white,
> I walked the ways and heard what all men said,
> Forests of tongues, like autumn leaves unshed,
> Being not unlovable but strange and light;
> Old riddles and new creeds, not in despite
> But softly, as men smile about the dead.

[2] Ibid., 321.

The sages have a hundred maps to give
That trace their crawling cosmos like a tree,
They rattle reason out through many a sieve
That stores the sand and lets the gold go free:
And all these things are less than dust to me
Because my name is Lazarus and I live.

In the book *The Catholic Church and Conversion*, Chesterton says that although all roads lead to Rome, each pilgrim is tempted to talk as if all roads had been like his own road. But "the Church is a house with a hundred gates; and no two men enter at exactly the same angle".[3] Still, while every conversion story is different, every conversion story is also the same. Chesterton recognizes that there are three stages that most every convert goes through on his road to Rome: The first stage is "patronising the Church; the second, discovering the Church; and the third, running away from the Church".[4]

It may surprise some to know that Chesterton was raised as a Unitarian universalist. When he first embraced Christianity, as described in his book *Orthodoxy*, he had indeed a very orthodox view of it. He joined the Church of England, which he says was simply his own uncompleted conversion to Catholicism. But since he was never really a Protestant, he never held any of the Protestant views toward Rome, that is to say, he was never really anti-Catholic. He did not have to deal with the same stumbling blocks many Protestant converts have to overcome on their way to Rome. The two main Protestant objections regard the Bible and the priesthood. Chesterton deals rather

---

[3] *The Catholic Church and Conversion*, *CW* 3:72.
[4] Ibid., 98.

handily with these. In the first place, Protestants are simply misinformed about what the Catholic view toward Scripture is. The usual protest of the Protestant is that the Church of Rome is afraid of the Bible. There are a couple of ironic things about this. First of all, says Chesterton,

> I grew up in a world in which the Protestants, who had just proved that Rome did not believe the Bible, were excitedly discovering that they did not believe the Bible themselves.[5]

Secondly, he says he could perhaps understand an outsider dismissing the Church altogether, saying that its scrolls and statues and rituals and candles were all "bosh", but he could not understand an outsider dismissing everything about the Church *except* the scrolls and to put faith only in the scrolls and to claim that the scrolls, which came from the Church, were against the Church.[6]

On the subject of priests, Chesterton responds to the Protestant accusations that priests are dangerous and unnatural and unholy men by saying here Protestants want to have it both ways. They think a priest is a fool for keeping his vows and a scoundrel for breaking them.

> Why should a man who wanted to be wicked encumber himself with special and elaborate promises to be good?[7]

Chesterton dismisses these and other Protestant pictures of Catholicism as "obvious blunders". The real reasons that prevent people from becoming Catholic are not the lies about the Catholic Church but, rather, the truth about it. There is a fear, not of the vices of the Church, but of its virtues. For example, the fear of the confessional. A religion that has, as

---

[5] Ibid., 71–72.
[6] Ibid., 73.
[7] Ibid., 74.

one of its foundations, the confessing of sins is a religion that deals in truth. The fear of course is unfounded, for the penitent finds that the confessional is a place of mercy and gigantic generosity.[8] Still, a very real fear remains of the Church's reality. This is a Church that tells us clearly to whom we are responsible and for what. The rest of the world finds such clarity not just uncomfortable, but frightening.

That fear is what the convert faces at the third stage of conversion, which is running away from the Church. That fear can be most intense when we know the facts rather than the falsehoods, and we know that the last step is entirely up to us. Before discussing this final step, let us briefly return to the first two stages of conversion: patronizing the Church and discovering the Church. The convert takes his first step rather unwittingly when he decides he is going to be "fair" to the Catholic Church. He does not think the Roman religion is true, but, for the first time, he also does not think that the accusations against the Church are true. He decides to make an objective investigation of the Catholic Church. This important first step leads to a long and enjoyable second step, which is the utter fascination of learning what the Catholic Church really does teach. Chesterton says this is the most pleasant part of the business,

> easier than joining the Catholic Church and much easier than trying to live the Catholic life. It is like discovering a new continent full of strange flowers and fantastic animals, which is at once wild and hospitable.[9]

But then the convert suddenly realizes with a shock that he can no longer be detached and impartial about the Catholic Church.

[8] Ibid., 87.
[9] Ibid., 91.

It is impossible to be just to the Catholic Church. The moment men cease to pull against it they feel a tug towards it. The moment they cease to shout it down they begin to listen to it with pleasure. The moment they try to be fair to it they begin to be fond of it. But when that affection has passed a certain point it begins to take on the tragic and menacing grandeur of a great love affair. The man has exactly the same sense of having committed or compromised himself; of having been in a sense entrapped, even if he is glad to be entrapped. But for a considerable time he is not so much glad as simply terrified. It may be that this real psychological experience has been ... responsible for all that remains of the legend that Rome is a mere trap. But that legend misses the whole point of the psychology. It is not the Pope who has set the trap or the priests who have baited it. The whole point of the position is that the trap is simply the truth. The whole point is that the man himself has made his way towards the trap of truth, and not the trap that has run after the man.[10]

We have said that Chesterton's conversion was gradual and deliberate, but as any convert knows, that last step is still a huge one. He says,

The space between doing and not doing such a thing is so tiny and so vast.... It is one thing to conclude that Catholicism is good and another to conclude that it is right. It is one thing to conclude that it is right and another to conclude that it is always right.[11]

It is indeed stepping out of one world and into another. And it is no small step. There is one more rather surprising thing that can prevent that final step. As a convert myself I can attest to the truth of what Chesterton means when he says:

[10] Ibid., 92.
[11] Ibid., 95.

There is many a convert who has reached a stage at which no word from any Protestant or pagan could any longer hold him back. Only the word of a Catholic can keep him from Catholicism.[12]

One foolish word from inside does more harm than a hundred thousand foolish words from outside.[13]

Catholics sometimes do a very poor job of presenting their faith, saying or doing or emphasizing the wrong thing, showing no appreciation or understanding either of the convert or of the faith. They are often more effective at keeping people away from the faith than its enemies are, because, as Chesterton says, its enemies are not really very effective at all.

When the convert finally does overcome all the obstacles of his own fear and ignorance, when he finally does take the final step, he then encounters the curious reactions of other people, who for some reason think that the fact that the convert has found peace of mind means that his mind has stopped working.

To become a Catholic is not to leave off thinking, but to learn how to think. It is so in exactly the same sense in which to recover from palsy is not to leave off moving but to learn how to move. The Catholic convert has for the first time a starting-point for straight and strenuous thinking. He has for the first time a way of testing the truth in any question that he raises. As the world goes, especially at present, it is the other people, the heathen and the heretics, who seem to have every virtue except the power of connected thought.... What is now called free thought is valued, not because it is free thought, but because it is freedom from thought; because it is free thoughtlessness....

[12] Ibid., 87–88.
[13] Ibid., 87.

The outsiders, stand by and see, or think they see, the convert entering with bowed head a sort of small temple which they are convinced is fitted up inside like a prison, if not a torture-chamber. But all they really know about it is that he has passed through a door. They do not know that he has not gone into the inner darkness, but out into the broad daylight.[14]

When [the convert] has entered the Church, he finds that the Church is much larger inside than it is outside.[15]

Chesterton says

The Catholic Church is the only thing which saves a man from the degrading slavery of being a child of his age.[16]

Every age seems bent on trying to create a new religion, but new religions are only suited to what is new. They "express one idea at a time, because that idea happens to be fashionable at the moment".[17] They profess to be progressive "because the peculiar boast of their peculiar period was progress; they claim to be democratic because our political system still rather pathetically claims to be democratic." They boast of a reconciliation with science, which is "often only a premature surrender to science". They get rid of anything that may look or seem "old-fashioned". They claim to have "bright services and cheery sermons". The churches compete with the cinemas; the churches even become cinemas.[18] But religions that are based on moods and fashions are not really religions at all. And, of course, because they are based on moods and fashions, they cannot last.

[14] Ibid., 106–7.
[15] Ibid., 94.
[16] Ibid., 110.
[17] Ibid., 108.
[18] Ibid., 111.

The Catholic Church, says Chesterton, "has all the freshness of a new religion", but it also has "all the richness of an
old religion".[19] It does not change with people's tastes. It is
a religion that binds men to their morality even when they
are not in the mood to be moral. The Church often has to
go against the grain of the world. It has preached social reconciliation to fierce and raging factions who would much
rather destroy each other. He says it preached charity to the
old pagans who did not believe in it, just as it now preaches
chastity to the new pagans who do not believe in it.[20]

> We do not really want a religion that is right where we are
> right. What we want is a religion that is right where we are
> wrong....[Some] people merely take the modern mood ...
> and then require any creed to be cut down to fit that mood.
> But the mood would exist even without the creed. They say
> they want a religion to be social, when they would be social
> without any religion. They say they want a religion to be
> practical, when they would be practical without any reli-
> gion. They say they want a religion acceptable to science,
> when they would accept the science even if they did not
> accept the religion. They say they want a religion like this
> because they are like this already. They say they want it, when
> they mean that they could do without it.[21]

People of course do not like to be told that there are certain
things they cannot do. They think that means they do not
have liberty. But Chesterton has already showed us in his
book *Orthodoxy* that freedom is something that only exists
within the rules. It is when you break the rules that you
become bound by the consequences. Chesterton finds this
idea confirmed in the Catholic Church. He finds it a place

[19] Ibid., 110.
[20] Ibid., 111.
[21] Ibid.

of enormous liberty. The vetoes are actually very few, but
they are very clear, and they only have our ultimate interests
in mind. We are obsessed with the forbidden fruit. But, Chesterton says, there is actually something fruitful about the forbidden fruit, "in the sense of a fascinating botanical study of
why it is really poisonous" [22] and why the Church is right to
forbid it. He says that the Church's rules are merely common sense.

> The fact remains that the Church is right in the main in
> being tolerant in the main; but that where she is intolerant
> she is most right and even more reasonable. Adam lived in a
> garden where a thousand mercies were granted to him; but
> the one inhibition was the greatest mercy of all. [23]

Chesterton finds that the Church has been "true all along",
true to the first and last things, true to our unspoiled instincts and our conclusive experience. It did not surrender
to fashion or to intellectual snobs. Because it has not sur-
rendered, the Church has the reputation for being behind
the times. In truth, it is usually ahead of the times. For instance, Chesterton found that his own ideas about economic
and social justice, which he came upon very slowly, had already been articulated by Pope Leo XIII, decades before him.
Pope Leo said, "As many as possible of the working classes
should become owners." [24] What Chesterton thought was a
new and urgent idea was already the position of the Catholic
Church.

It is worth repeating:

> The Catholic Church is the only thing which saves a man
> from the degrading slavery of being a child of his age.

---

[22] Ibid., 119.
[23] Ibid.
[24] Quoted in ibid., 114.

Slavery. To associate the Church with freedom, and every other religion and philosophy with slavery, is a startling and striking idea. But Chesterton does not make the statement merely for its shock effect. He speaks from his own experience. In the Church he found freedom. The truth does set you free. He says if he ever left the Church, it would mean giving up his freedom.

> I could no more go back to those cushioned chapels than a man who has regained his sanity would willingly go back to a padded cell.... I know that Catholicism is too large for me, and I have not yet explored its beautiful and terrible truths. But I know that Universalism is too small for me; and I could not creep back into that dull safety, who have looked on the dizzy vision of liberty.[25]

Chesterton ends the book with an interesting postscript. He notes that there were quite a few conversions at the time. He does not know the statistics, but he says statistics are misleading anyway. The point is, he was a convert, and he knew of many others. He knew of the reality of conversion. At the same time, he notes that a number of people were leaving the Church, and he also notes the reason they were leaving was not the Church's creed but its moral restraints. But he says that he actually has "more sympathy with the person who leaves the Church for a love-affair than with one who leaves it for a long-winded German theory to prove that God is evil or that children are a sort of morbid monkey".[26]

In other words, it is not a controversy between two defined philosophies, but, as he says, a controversy between philosophers and philanderers. As such, he is not worried about the outcome of the battle between those who have

---

[25] Ibid., 120.
[26] Ibid., 123.

stayed and those who have scattered. There will always be people who quarrel with the Church's moral teaching. Chesterton might be surprised to know that today, they do not want to leave the Church but to remain members and try to change the Church's teaching to accommodate their own bad ideas or bad morals. And yet, the prophetic comment that ends the book is still true and is both troubling and hopeful at the same time. He says, at worst, there will be "a battle between bad Catholics and good Catholics, with the great dome over all".[27]

[27] Ibid., 124.

6

The Thing: Why I Am a Catholic

> The mind must be enlarged to see the simple things; or
> even to see the self-evident things.... It never occurs to
> the critic to do anything so simple as to compare what is
> Catholic with what is Non-Catholic. The one thing that
> never seems to cross his mind, when he argues about what
> the Church is like, is the simple question of what the world
> would be like without it.
>
> — *The Thing*

In 1929, Chesterton published a collection of essays under
the very suggestive title *The Thing*. (Modern editions of the
book have added the subtitle, "Why I Am a Catholic", which
is the title of one of the essays in the book.) What is "The
Thing"? It is not just any thing. It is not just another thing.
It is *The* Thing.

It is the Catholic Church.

In this book Chesterton compares "The Thing" to all other
things: worldly philosophies, business, nationalism, Protes-
tantism, agnosticism, art, history, education, and even sports.
The word "catholic" means "universal", and in this book
Chesterton shows how The Thing applies to everything else.
He also shows how The Thing is opposed by everything

else. The attacks on the Catholic faith come from all sides. Chesterton notes that "religious tolerance" seems to mean that liberal and large-minded Christians see good in all religions and nothing but evil in the Catholic Church. He not only defends the Church from a great variety of attacks, he shows how it is the right solution to all the world's dilemmas. In every case, the Catholic position is one of common sense. "The Faith", he says, "gives a man back his body and his soul and his reason and his will and his very life." [1]

Chesterton says that all the revolts against the Church, from even before the Reformation until now, tell the same strange story.

> Every great heretic had always exhibited three remarkable characteristics in combination. First, he picked out some mystical idea from the Church's ... balance of mystical ideas. Second, he used that one mystical idea against all the other mystical ideas. Third (and most singular), he seems generally to have had no notion that his own favourite mystical idea was a mystical idea, at least in the sense of a mysterious or dubious or dogmatic idea. [2]

Thus, Calvinists are obsessed only with the sovereignty of God, Lutherans with the grace of God, Methodists with the sin of man, Baptists with the Bible, Quakers with simplicity. The list goes on; it even includes religious and political movements outside of Christianity. Muslims are obsessed with the Oneness of God, communists with the equality of men, feminists with the equality of men and women, materialists with creation apart from the Creator, spiritualists with the rejection of materialism, and so on. In every case, these sects have

---

[1] *The Thing, CW* 3:145.
[2] Ibid., 152.

taken one of the Church's mystical ideas and exalted it above the rest, even against the rest. They have lost all the moderating and balancing measures of The Thing, the Catholic faith.

What is more, Chesterton says, the modern world, with its modern movements,

> is living on its Catholic capital. It is using, and using up, the truths that remain to it out of the old treasury of Christendom.[3]

The modern world may claim to have new ideas, but they are not new at all. They are borrowed piecemeal from the past. The modern world

> is not starting fresh things that it can really carry on far into the future. On the contrary, it is picking up old things that it cannot carry on at all.[4]

He says these are the two marks of modern moral ideals.

> First, that they were borrowed or snatched out of ancient or mediaeval hands. Second, that they wither very quickly in modern hands.[5]

There are timeless truths imbedded in Catholic traditions, but the modern world either attacks the traditions it does not keep or misuses and misunderstands the traditions it does keep. The result is a weak mixture of unworkable schemes that undermine our society, our families, and our very souls.

[3] Ibid., 147.
[4] Ibid.
[5] Ibid.

Chesterton says we have fallen into "a habit of mere drift and gradual detachment from family life".[6] It may be accidental, but it is nonetheless anarchical.

> Some social reformers try to evade this difficulty, I know, by some vague notions about the State or an abstraction called Education eliminating the parental function.... It is based on that strange new superstition, the idea of infinite resources of organization. It is as if officials grew like grass or bred like rabbits. There is supposed to be an endless supply of salaried persons, and of salaries for them; and they are to undertake all that human beings naturally do for themselves; including the care of children.... The actual effect of this theory is that one harassed person has to look after a hundred children, instead of one normal person looking after a normal number of them. Normally that normal person is urged by a natural force, which costs nothing and does not require a salary; the force of natural affection for his young, which exists even among the animals. If you cut off that natural force, and substitute a paid bureaucracy, you are like a ... lunatic who should carefully water his garden with a watering-can, while holding up an umbrella to keep off the rain.[7]

> The truly extraordinary suggestion is often made that this escape from the home is an escape into greater freedom.... To anybody who can think, of course, it is exactly the opposite.... [T]he world *outside* the home is now under a rigid discipline and routine and it is only inside the home that there is really a place for individuality and liberty.... Business, especially big business, is now organized like an army.... The pursuit of pleasure is merely the pursuit of fashion. The

[6] Ibid., 158.
[7] Ibid., 160.

pursuit of fashion is merely the pursuit of convention. . . .
But it is the enjoyment of convention, not the enjoyment of
liberty.[8]

Chesterton argues that the place of greatest liberty is the home
and that the worst thing about this drift away from the home
is that it is simply unintelligent.

People do not know what they are doing; because they do
not know what they are undoing.[9]

Thus, it is now necessary to repeat things that we all know
are true but which we have apparently forgotten. We have
forgotten the very *reasons* for the existence of the family. He
says,

They were all familiar to our fathers, who believed in the
links of kinship and also in the links of logic. Today our logic
consists mostly of missing links; and our family largely of
absent members.[10]

Chesterton's logic, on the other hand, has no missing links.
It is utterly connected and utterly consistent. And it is refreshing. It is the clean strong breeze of common sense. Not
surprisingly, it exactly reflects the Church's position.

I actually prefer weddings to divorces and babies to Birth
Control. These eccentric views, which I share with the over-
whelming majority of mankind, past and present, I should
not attempt to defend here one by one. . . . I wish to make it
unmistakably plain that my defence of these sentiments is
not sentimental. . . .

[8] Ibid., 161–62.
[9] Ibid., 164.
[10] Ibid., 160.

On the contrary, it is the sceptics who are the sentimentalists.... We can always convict such people of sentimentalism by their weakness for euphemism. The phrase they use is always softened and suited for journalistic appeals. They talk of free love when they mean something quite different, better defined as free lust. But being sentimentalists they feel bound to simper and coo over the word "love." They insist on talking about Birth Control when they mean less birth and no control. We could smash them to atoms, if we could be as indecent in our language as they are immoral in their conclusions.[11]

According to Chesterton, the modern world's weakness for euphemism is evidence of a mental breakdown even more than of a moral breakdown. When we use language, not to express the truth, but to disguise the truth, we soon lose our ability to think clearly. It was this mental breakdown, this twisting of words and their meanings, that paved the way to today's obvious moral breakdown. Chesterton saw it before it was obvious. And he clearly understood and explained the mental breakdown that precedes the moral breakdown. That is probably why the modern world has found it so convenient to forget Chesterton. Today's intellectual establishment does not want to engage a clear thinker like G. K. Chesterton in an actual argument. They do not want controversies settled by argument. They especially do not like the idea of yielding to common sense. Still, we must not be afraid to pick up the argument where Chesterton left off. It is still the same argument, still the same truth that needs to be defended. Chesterton still cheers us on. He says, by way of encouragement,

[11] Ibid., 169–70.

We are not entitled to despair of explaining the truth; nor is
it really so horribly difficult to explain.[12]

In this book and in all his writings, Chesterton shows that
he is not afraid to take on the most difficult and controversial
issues, for instance, evolution. He says that evolution as an
explanation does not explain anything. As for the idea of
natural selection and "survival of the fittest", if it means only
that things fitted for survival do in fact survive, well, that
does not really give you much actual information. Nobody
needs to be told that in a flood fish live and cattle die. The
question is: How soon do cattle turn into fish? Is there a
logical explanation for this? As Chesterton says, our logic
consists mostly of missing links.

A related question is: Was there a Garden of Eden, and
was there a Fall?

Whether or no the garden was an allegory, the truth itself
can be very well allegorized as a garden. And the point of it
is that Man, whatever else he is, is certainly *not* merely one
of the plants of the garden that has plucked its roots out of
the soil and walked about with them like legs.... He is something else, something strange and solitary.[13]

Chesterton says that the Fall is actually an encouraging view
of life. It means "that happiness is not only a hope, but also
in some strange manner a memory; and that we are all kings
in exile".[14] It is much more encouraging to realize that we
have misused a good world rather than that we are merely
trapped in a bad one. It is more encouraging that evil has to

[12] Ibid., 237.
[13] Ibid., 310–11.
[14] Ibid., 312.

do with the wrong use of the will, which means it can eventually be righted by a right use of the will.

Every other creed ... is some form of surrender to fate.[15]

This is certainly true of the Calvinist idea of predestination. Broadly speaking, there are only two views on the subject of God's foreknowledge of what we will do with our lives: the Catholic view and the Calvinist view. The Catholic believes that God knows, as a fact, that I choose to go to the devil. The Calvinist believes that God has given me to the devil, without my having any choice at all. Chesterton says that if a man believes in God at all, he would "certainly prefer a God who has made all men for joy, and desires to save them all" and gives them the opportunity to be saved, as opposed to "a God who deliberately made some for involuntary sin and immortal misery".[16] How is the newer Calvinist idea an improvement over the older Catholic idea?

Chesterton says that modern thinkers will not follow new ideas to their logical end; nor will they trace traditional ideas back to their beginnings. If they followed the new notions forward it would lead them to nonsense or utter chaos. If they followed their better instincts backward, it would lead them to Rome. So they refuse to follow either one and remain suspended between two logical alternatives and try to tell themselves that they are merely avoiding extremes.

Our critics, in condemning us, always argue in a circle. They say of mediaevalism that all men were narrow. When they discover that many of them were very broad, they insist that those men must have been in revolt, not only against mediaevalism, but against Catholicism. No Catholics were intel-

15 Ibid., 311.
16 Ibid., 186.

ligent; for when they were intelligent, they cannot really have
been Catholics.[17]

Ours is ... the most rational of all religions.... Those who
talk about it as merely ... emotional simply do not know
what they are talking about. It is ... all the modern religions, that are merely emotional.... We alone are left ac-
cepting the action of the reason and the will without any
necessary assistance from the emotions. A convinced Catholic is easily the most ... logical person walking about the
world today.[18]

Freethinkers are occasionally thoughtful, though never free.
In the modern world of the West ... they seem always to be
tied to the treadmill of a materialist and monist cosmos....
The freethinker is not free to question monism. He is forbidden ... to believe in a miracle.... We [Catholics] are the
freer of the two; as there is scarcely any evidence, natural or
preternatural, that cannot be accepted as fitting into our system somewhere; whereas the materialist cannot fit the most
minute miracle into his system anywhere.[19]

Chesterton says that the freethinker, though not free, is at
least a better thinker than many, shall we say, "half-washed"
skeptics. A person who rejects the faith altogether is more
consistent than a person who rejects just parts of the faith,
keeping the parts that please him, tossing the parts that puzzle him. A perfect example of the latter would be the great
American lawyer and skeptic Clarence Darrow, whom Chesterton once met in a debate.

Mr. Clarence Darrow, the somewhat simple-minded sceptic
of that land of simplicity ... seems to have been writing

---

[17] Ibid., 262.
[18] Ibid., 286.
[19] Ibid., 305.

something about the impossibility of anybody having a soul. . . .
[He] thinks of the soul superstitiously, as a separate and secret animal with wings; . . . [as something] quite apart from
the self. . . . One of his arguments against immortality is that
people do not really believe in it. . . . If they did believe in
certain happiness beyond the grave, they would all kill
themselves. . . .

Now there we have the final flower and crown of all modern optimism and universalism and humanitarianism in religion. Sentimentalists talk about love till the world is sick of
the most glorious of all human words; they assume that there
is nothing in the next world except the sort of Utopia of
practical pleasure which they promise us (but do not give us)
in this world. They declare that all will be forgiven, because
there is nothing to forgive. They insist that "passing over" is
only like going into the next room. . . . They are positive that
there is no danger, no devil; even no death. All is hope, happiness and optimism. And . . . the logical result of all that
hope, happiness and optimism would be hundreds of people
hanging from lamp-posts or thousands of people throwing
themselves into wells or canals. We should find the rational
result of the modern Religion of Joy and Love in one huge
human stampede of suicide. . . .

Now, of course, . . . a Catholic does not kill himself because he does not take it for granted that he will deserve
heaven in any case, . . . or at all. He does not profess to know
exactly what danger he would run; but he does know what
loyalty he would violate and what command . . . he would
disregard. He actually thinks that a man might be fitter for
heaven because he endured like a man; and that a hero could
be a martyr to cancer as St. Lawrence or St. Cecilia were
martyrs to cauldrons or gridirons. The faith in a future life,
the hope of a future happiness, the belief that God is Love
and that loyalty is eternal life, these things do not produce
lunacy and anarchy, *if* they are taken along with other Catholic doctrines about duty and vigilance and watchfulness

against the powers of hell. They might produce lunacy and anarchy, if they were taken alone. And the Modernists, that is, the optimists and sentimentalists, did want us to take them alone. Of course the same would be true, if somebody took the other doctrines of duty and discipline alone. It would produce another dark age of Puritans rapidly blackening into Pessimists. Indeed, the extremes meet, when they are both ends clipped off what should be a complete thing. Our parable ends poetically with ... the suicidal pessimist and ... the suicidal optimist....

The Catholic has an extremely simple and sensible reason for not cutting his throat in order to fly instantly into Paradise. But he might really raise a question for those who talk as if Paradise were invariably and instantly populated with people who had cut their throats.[20]

Chesterton also deals with one of most common attacks against the Catholic Church: the charge of corruption. He says the point about corruption is that only a good thing can become corrupted. A corrupt thing cannot become corrupted.[21] And if corruption continues unabated, it destroys what it corrupts. But the Catholic Church has lasted two thousand years. Certainly at the time of the Reformation, there were instances of the Church being too worldly, but Chesterton says the worst things in worldly Catholicism were made much worse by the revolt against the Church.[22]

As one example, the revolt against confession eventually gave us something much worse than confession: psychotherapy, which is confession without absolution and without any of the safeguards of the confessional.[23] Chesterton says,

[20] Ibid., 306–8.
[21] Ibid., 232.
[22] Ibid., 186.
[23] Ibid., 187.

If a girl must not mention sin to a man in a corner of a church, it is apparently the only place nowadays in which she may not do so.[24]

Chesterton frankly admits that throughout history many Catholics have failed to live up to the Catholic ideals, "but", he says, "many more modern men are more disastrously failing in the attempt to live without them."[25] And finally, he says the world really pays the supreme compliment to the Catholic Church when the world will not tolerate even the appearance of evil in the Church when the same world tolerates it everywhere else.[26] In other words, the world will ignore its own failures but will not abide the idea that the Church could ever be as bad as the world. The world knows The Thing is the truth.

There has to be one truth that holds all other truths together. Chesterton uses the image of a broken stained-glass window, which is the present state of the world.[27] We can pick up the pieces, but what can put everything back together? What is the glue that makes religion both corporate and popular? What is the glue that will prevent the world from falling to pieces again in a debris of individual tastes? Chastity without humility. Humility without chastity. Truth and beauty without either and without each other. What is the thing that can contain everything and hold it all together? Well, that is just The Thing.

[24] Ibid., 273.
[25] Ibid., 235.
[26] Ibid., 275.
[27] Ibid., 156.

7

The Well and the Shallows

We need not deny that modern doubt, like ancient doubt, does ask deep questions; we only deny that ... it gives any deeper answers. And it is a general rule, touching what is called modern thought, that while the questions are often really deep, the answers are often decidedly shallow. And it is perhaps even more important to remark that, while the questions are in a sense eternal, the answers are in every sense ephemeral.

— *The Well and the Shallows*

In his classic book *Orthodoxy*, Chesterton wrote, "Thinking means connecting things."[1] And that is exactly what he does in his collection of essays called *The Well and the Shallows*. In this book, Chesterton makes startling connections between things: between capitalism and sex, between Protestantism and fossils, between skepticism and soap, between commercialism and rotten apples. *The Well and the Shallows* was published in 1935, and it could easily be called *More of the Thing*, because once again, Chesterton connects "The Thing" to everything

[1] *Orthodoxy, CW* 1:238.

else. "The Thing" is the Catholic faith, which is not just a religious doctrine but a complete and integrated world view. Chesterton argues that all other religious, political, and social ideas are not only enemies of the Church but enemies of mankind. He shows how the Catholic faith provides the basis not only for our worship, but also for everything else. Nothing else provides the deep answers for the deep questions. The Catholic Church is the Well. Everything else is the Shallows.

In the book, Chesterton gives a number of reasons why, after considering several other religions, philosophies, and political theories and discovering how flimsy and fleeting they are, he *would* have converted to Catholicism except for one problem: he already had.

All other systems at some point and in some way attack the idea of free will. And when they attack free will, they attack human dignity. One of the reasons for Chesterton's greatness is that he always defends freedom and dignity. He argues that nothing is inevitable. We need never surrender to this or that set of circumstances, to social forces, to biological determinism, to history, or to fate. This is the essence of freedom. Modern man thinks freedom means breaking the rules, but, as Chesterton points out, freedom means exercising free will to obey the rules. Without freedom there is no such thing as obedience and responsibility. We are not forced to obey. We choose. That is what gives us our dignity. We make a vow by choice. Freedom means keeping the vow, no matter how difficult, not breaking it, no matter how compelling.

The world, of course, thinks that a person who becomes Catholic gives up his liberty. But, as Chesterton says,

> Tell a Catholic convert that he has lost his liberty, and he will laugh.[2]

---

[2] *The Well and the Shallows*, CW 3:372.

THE WELL AND THE SHALLOWS

This book is largely a defense of liberty and an attack on its enemies. The progressives, the reactionaries, the socialists, the capitalists, all appeal to trends and inevitabilities. Some insist that the world is getting better. Others insist that the world is getting worse. But Chesterton says what the world does is wobble.

> Life in itself is not a ladder; it is a see-saw.[3]

This is basically what the Church has always said. There are wrongs that can be righted and that should be righted. But there is no certainty that they *will* be righted. The Church tells us we must not count on the certainty of comforts becoming more common or cruelties more rare, as if there were an inevitable trend toward a sinless humanity:

> We must not hate humanity, or despise humanity, or refuse to help humanity; but we must not trust humanity.[4]

When Chesterton says we must not trust humanity, he especially reminds us not to put too much trust in politics or in whatever political party we pick. We generally expect too much from political parties, but none of them is based on any permanent philosophy, and, because of that, at some point they will conflict with the faith.

A Catholic would be especially wise not to put too much faith in anything other than the faith. A Catholic should resist the fleeting philosophies and the ephemeral ideas offered by any social movement or political party or anything else.

Certainly we should be wise enough not to put our trust in "progress". Progress cannot say what it is. It is detached from any eternal goals. It is purely pragmatic and ultimately immoral. And Chesterton predicts in this book, written in

[3] Ibid., 364.
[4] Ibid.

1935, that the march of *progress* will lead us through contra-ception to abortion and to infanticide.[5] He also seems to be describing the present state of things when he says,

> One of the chief features of the state of Peace we now enjoy is the killing of a considerable number of harmless human beings.[6]

There are many other prophetic comments in this book. He anticipates the trend of our popular entertainment to the ever bigger, bolder, louder, and more shocking. He says,

> The nerve is being killed; and it is being killed by being overstimulated and therefore stunted and stunned.[7]

He also rightly predicts that people would appeal to "con-science" as the supreme authority and use it to justify every ill-conceived idea. And he argues,

> Why should your conscience be any more reliable than your rotting teeth or your quite special defect of eyesight?[8]

A Catholic appeals to something much higher and more trust-worthy than conscience. "A Catholic", says Chesterton, "is a person who has plucked up courage to face the incredible and inconceivable idea that something else may be wiser than he is."[9]

The Church proclaims the truth. Those who reject the Church would like truth to conform to their own desires. They will not admit the truth, which is something much

[5] Ibid., 530.
[6] Ibid., 415.
[7] Ibid., 416.
[8] Ibid., 394.
[9] Ibid., 369.

greater than themselves. They will not only disobey the truth, they will attack it.

> What is really working in the world today is Anti-Catholicism and nothing else. It certainly is not Protestantism.[10]

> Protestantism is now only a name; but it is a name that can be used to cover any or every "ism" except Catholicism. It is now a vessel or receptacle into which can be poured all the thousand things that for a thousand reasons react against Rome; but it can only be full of these things ... because it is itself empty. Every sort of negation, every sort of new religion, every sort of moral revolt or intellectual irritation, that can make a man resist the claim of the Catholic Faith, is here gathered into a heap and covered with a convenient but quite antiquated label.[11]

What is replacing this hollow thing called Protestantism is paganism, which is "a thing more attractive because it appears to be more human than any of the heresies."

> The Pagan looks for his pleasures to the natural forces of this world; but ... the natural forces, when they are turned into gods, betray mankind by something that is in the very nature of nature-worship. We can already see men becoming unhealthy by the worship of health; becoming hateful by the worship of love; becoming paradoxically solemn and overstrained even by the idolatry of sport; and in some cases strangely morbid and infected with horrors by the perversion of a just sympathy with animals.... There is nothing in Paganism to check its own exaggerations.[12]

Chesterton says that the only thing that can check the exaggerations of paganism is a return to Thomistic philosophy,

[10] Ibid., 464.
[11] Ibid., 469.
[12] Ibid., 473–74.

because it is the philosophy of common sense. Compared with all other philosophies, the Roman religion is the only rationalistic religion. The materialist says that the soul does not exist; a new kind of mystic says that the body does not exist. The Scholastic is needed to explain the simple, rational truth that both exist. The other philosophies are an attack not only on common sense, but also on reality.

> To say that there is no pain, or no matter, or no evil, or no difference between man and beast, or indeed between anything and anything else—this is a desperate effort to destroy all experience and sense of reality.[13]

The modern world has been one long rebellion against the traditional, commonsense teachings of the Church. And those who rebel achieve precisely the opposite effect of what they claim.

> Those who leave the tradition of truth do not escape into something which we call Freedom. They only escape into something else, which we call Fashion.... The little group of Atheists ... began their agitation in the old Victorian days.... They did not call themselves Atheists, they called themselves Secularists.... [But] the word "secular" does not mean anything so sensible as "worldly." It does not even mean anything so spirited as "irreligious." To be secular simply means to be of the age; that is, of the age which is passing; of the age which, in their case, is already passed.... There is one adequate equivalent of the word "secular"; and it is the word "dated."[14]

Chesterton also rightly predicts that the moderns would rebel against modernism. When progressives come to the edge of

---

[13] Ibid., 475.
[14] Ibid., 388–89.

the precipice, it is only the people behind them who are still shouting "Forward!"

"The Modern Mind", he says, "is not at all accustomed to making up its mind." [15] And modern intellectuals ("for want of a more intellectual term", says Chesterton), while unable to make up their own minds, would like to make up everyone else's mind. On the one hand, they would like to force social programs on common people that would deprive them of their freedom. On the other hand, they would like to do away with basic moral truths, calling the resulting anarchy "freedom", and thereby deprive people of their dignity.

> There are not many things which move me to anything like a personal contempt. I do not feel any contempt for an atheist, who is often a man limited and constrained by his own logic to a very sad simplification. I do not feel any contempt for a Bolshevist, who is a man driven to the same negative simplification by a revolt against very positive wrongs. But there is one type of person for whom I feel what I can only call contempt. And that is the popular propagandist of what he or she absurdly describes as Birth-Control.
>
> I despise Birth-Control first because it is a weak and wobbly and cowardly word. It is also an entirely meaningless word; and is used so as to curry favour even with those who would at first recoil from its real meaning. The proceeding these quack doctors recommend does not *control* any birth. It only makes sure that there shall never be any birth to control. . . . But these people know perfectly well that they dare not write the plain word Birth-Prevention ... where they write the hypocritical word Birth-Control. They know as well as I do that the very word Birth-Prevention would strike a chill into the public. . . .

[15] Ibid., 389.

Second, I despise Birth-Control because it is a weak and wobbly and cowardly thing.[16]

But ... my contempt boils over into bad behaviour when I hear the common suggestion that a birth is avoided because people want to be "free" to go to the cinema or buy a gramophone or a loud-speaker. What makes me want to walk over such people like doormats is that they use the word "free." By every act of that sort they chain themselves to the most servile and mechanical system yet tolerated by men. The cinema ... [and] the gramophone ... [and] the loud-speaker [are part of the] central mechanism giving out to men exactly what their masters think they should have.

Now a child is the very sign and sacrament of personal freedom. He is a fresh free will added to the wills of the world; he is something that his parents have freely chosen to produce and ... freely agree to protect. They can feel that any amusement he gives (which is often considerable) really comes from him and from them, and from nobody else. He has been born without the intervention of any master or lord. He is a creation and a contribution; he is their own creative contribution to creation. He is also a much more beautiful, wonderful, amusing and astonishing thing than any of the stale stories or ... tunes turned out by the machines.... People who prefer the mechanical pleasures, to such a miracle, are jaded and enslaved. They are preferring the very dregs of life to the first fountains of life.... It is they who are hugging the chains of their old slavery; it is the child who is ready for the new world.[17]

Chesterton says that the modern sin of sex differs from the ancient sin of sex, and the ancient sin of sex actually was not as bad because

[16] Ibid., 439.
[17] Ibid., 440–41.

it was ... interwoven, very closely, with the cult of ... Fruit-fulness.... It was at least on the side of Nature. It was at least on the side of Life.[18]

But the moderns have invented a new kind of worship; a worship of sex, and one that is not even a worship of life. It is one "which at once exalts lust and forbids fertility." [19]

Just as sex has been separated from fertility and become perverted, Chesterton says there has been a similar separation and perversion about the nature of property. The problem is that when moderns think of property,

they only think of it in the sense of Money; in the sense of salary; in the sense of something which is immediately consumed, enjoyed and expended; something which gives momentary pleasure and disappears. They do not understand that we mean by Property something that includes that pleasure incidentally; but begins and ends with something far more grand and worthy and creative. The man who ... owns the orchard ... does also enjoy the taste of apples; and let us hope, also, the taste of cider. But he is doing something very much grander, and ultimately more gratifying, than merely eating an apple. He is ... asserting that his soul is his own, and does not belong to the Orchard Survey Department, or the chief Trust in the Apple Trade. But he is also ... worshipping the fruitfulness of the world. Now the notion of narrowing property merely to *enjoying* money is exactly like the notion of narrowing love merely to *enjoying* sex. In both cases an incidental, isolated, servile and even secretive pleasure is substituted for participation in a great creative process; even in the everlasting Creation of the world.[20]

---

[18] Ibid., 501.
[19] Ibid., 501–2.
[20] Ibid., 502–3.

Whether we are talking about the fruitfulness of orchards or of people, Chesterton says, "The real habitation of Liberty is the home."[21] Everything in the modern world—our entertainment, our literature, our newspapers—tries to cover up this truth.

> If individuals have any hope of protecting their freedom, they must protect their family life.[22]

That is why Chesterton defends widespread property ownership, the idea that each family has a place to call its own, a place wherein to protect itself. Here, as elsewhere, he shows how the two great enemies of property—and of the family— are big government and big business.

> The State did not own men so entirely, even when it could send them to the stake, as it sometimes does now where it can send them to the elementary school.[23]

But, surprisingly, Chesterton says, what has done more to destroy the family in the modern world, even before the State got in on the act, is a rampant and unbridled capitalism. It is capitalism that has taken women out of the home and put them into commercial competition with men. It is capitalism that has destroyed the influence of the parent in favor of the employer. And it is capitalism that has driven people off the land and into the cities, making them more attached to their factories or their firms than to their families.

The problem, he says, is that "Trade has been put in place of Truth."[24] Trade, which is in its nature a secondary or dependent thing, has been elevated to a primary and inde-

[21] Ibid., 508.
[22] Ibid.
[23] Ibid., 507.
[24] Ibid., 496.

pendent thing; as an absolute. We are no longer concerned about the Good, but about the Goods.

> In all normal civilisations the trader existed and must exist. But in all normal civilisations the trader was the exception; certainly he was never the rule; and most certainly he was never the ruler. The predominance which he has gained in the modern world is the cause of all the disasters of the modern world. The universal habit of humanity has been to produce and consume as part of the same process; largely conducted by the same people in the same place.... Most of the people, for most of the time, were thinking about growing food and then eating it; not entirely about growing food and selling it at the stiffest price to somebody who had nothing to eat.[25]

Chesterton says there is no way out of the modern tangle, except for independent people and independent families to live simpler lives. That means learning how to be content with less, so that we can be more content. To be content is to be free. We are now caught up in system that is designed to keep us discontented and unsatisfied. A society that is "commercial and nothing else" is not a society based on contentment. It is not solid. Chesterton says,

> [Nothing solid can be built] upon the utterly unphilosophical philosophy of blind buying and selling; of bullying people into purchasing what they do not want; of making it badly so that they may break it and imagine they want it again; of keeping rubbish in rapid circulation like a duststorm in a desert; and pretending that you are teaching men to hope.[26]

[25] Ibid., 497–98.
[26] Ibid., 500.

Capitalism can be as materialistic a philosophy as communism and can never provide the basis for human happiness. Nor can any other system. Except one. In one of the most remarkable observations in the book, Chesterton says there are no fascists; there are no socialists; there are no liberals; there are no parliamentarians. In the place of all of them there is only the Church, "the one supremely inspiring and irritating institution in the world."[27] There is only the Church and its enemies. And its enemies are ready to be for or against violence, for or against liberty, for or against representative government, and even for or against peace.[28] He says that all the things that have come forward to try to take the place of the Church, to do its work, have instead tied themselves into knots and cannot do anything. The heresies decay and destroy themselves. Anything less than the Catholic faith is narrow and shallow and ultimately barren. But "we have come out of the shallows and the dry places to the one deep well; and the Truth is at the bottom of it."[29]

[27] Ibid., 385–86.
[28] Ibid., 386.
[29] Ibid., 391.

8

St. Francis of Assisi

> The modern mind is hard to please.... It calls any moral
> method unpractical, when it has just called any practical
> method immoral. But ... St. Francis was far from being
> ... fanatical or ... unpractical.... It was the whole mean-
> ing of his message that such mysticism makes a man cheer-
> ful and humane.... The whole point of his point of view
> was that it looked out freshly upon a fresh world, that
> might have been made that morning.
>
> — *St. Francis of Assisi*

Even in the modern world St. Francis of Assisi is one of the
most popular and admired of the saints. He is also one of the
most misunderstood. But there was one modern writer who
understood him very well: G. K. Chesterton.

In 1924, less than two years after his conversion to Catholicism, G. K. Chesterton wrote a book on St. Francis of
Assisi. Chesterton had always been attracted to St. Francis.
In fact, one of his earliest essays,[1] published long before his
conversion, was an appreciation of St. Francis. Indeed, he

---

[1] "Francis", *Twelve Types* (London: Arthur L. Humphreys, 1903).

says that St. Francis stands on a bridge connecting Chesterton's early life to his later conversion and beyond. He says that throughout his pilgrimage, Francis was never a stranger to him.[2]

In this wonderful book, Chesterton describes St. Francis first as a soldier and a fighter. Then as a builder and a reformer. Then a jester, a clown of God, a troubadour, and a poet. Then as a beggar, who embraced poverty as other men embrace wealth, a little poor man, who embraced not only all men as his brothers, but all creatures great and small. And finally, Chesterton describes Francis as a mirror of Christ, one who truly reflected the light of truth.

It may seem strange to think of St. Francis of Assisi as a soldier. But that was what he first wanted to be. There was nothing dishonorable about it. On the contrary, it was an act of chivalry. He was a patriot, and he believed in defending his own city of Assisi. He rode off to battle in a war with Perugia and expected to return a hero and a prince. But he was captured, and, instead of a prince, he was a prisoner.

Francis resolved to keep up the spirits of his fellow captives. He seems to have liked everybody—especially those whom everybody disliked him for liking. In fact, says Chesterton, it might have been while he was a prisoner that he "heard the first whisper of that wild blessing that afterwards took the form of a blasphemy; 'He listens to those to whom God himself will not listen.' "[3] He vowed never to refuse to help a poor man. "His life", says Chesterton, "was one riot of rash vows; of rash vows that turned out right."[4]

---

[2] *St. Francis of Assisi, CW* 2:31.
[3] Ibid., 52.
[4] Ibid., 48.

Francis trailed back ... to Assisi, a very dismal and disappointed and perhaps even derided figure.... It was his first descent into a dark ravine that is called the valley of humiliation.... He was also very much puzzled and bewildered.... He was riding listlessly in some wayside place ... when he saw a figure coming ... towards him and halted; for he saw it was a leper. And he knew instantly that his courage was challenged.... What he saw advancing was not the banner and spears of Perugia, from which it never occurred to him to shrink.... Francis Bernardone saw his fear coming up the road towards him; the fear that comes from within and not without.... Then he sprang from his horse ... and rushed on the leper and threw his arms round him.... To this man he gave what money he could and mounted and rode on. We do not know how far he rode, ... but it is said that when he looked back, he could see no figure on the road.[5]

Next comes the great "break" in the life of Francis of Assisi; the point at which something happened to him that Chesterton says "must remain greatly dark to most of us, who are ordinary and selfish men whom God has not broken to make anew." [6]

There was an old shrine in Assisi, the Church of St. Damian, which was neglected and falling to pieces. During the dark and aimless days following the tragic collapse of his military ambitions, Francis was in the habit of praying before the crucifix at St. Damian. One day he heard a voice saying to him:

"Francis, seest thou not that my house is in ruins? Go and restore it for me."

[5] Ibid., 55–56.
[6] Ibid., 57.

Francis sprang up and went ... to sell his own horse and ... several bales of his father's cloth, making the sign of the cross over them to indicate their pious and charitable destination. [His father] did not see things in this light.... He ... put his son under lock and key as a vulgar thief.... It was [Francis'] blackest moment; the whole world had turned over; the whole world was on top of him....

[The bishop] told Francis that he must unquestionably restore the money to his father; that no blessing could follow a good work done by unjust methods.... There was a new air about Francis....

He stood up before them all and said, "... I am a servant of God. Not only the money but everything that can be called his I will restore to my father, even the very clothes he has given me." And he rent off all his garments except one; and they saw that that was a hair-shirt....

He ... went out half-naked into the winter woods, walking the frozen ground between the frosty trees; a man without a father. He was penniless, he was parentless, he was to all appearance without a trade or a plan or a hope in the world; and as he went under the frosty trees, he burst suddenly into song....

He realised that the way to build a church is ... not to pay for it, certainly not with somebody else's money.... The way to build a church is to build it.

He went about by himself collecting stones. He begged all the people he met to give him stones. In fact he became a new sort of beggar, reversing the parable; a beggar who asks not for bread but a stone.... The very queerness of the request gave it a sort of popularity.... He worked with his own hands at the rebuilding of the church.... He was labouring at a double task, and rebuilding something else as well as the church of St. Damian ... something that has often enough fallen into ruin but has never been past rebuilding; a church that could always be built anew though it had

rotted away to its first foundation-stone, against which the
gates of hell shall not prevail. . . .

   The adoration of Christ had been a part of the man's pas-
sionate nature for a long time past. But the imitation of Christ
. . . may . . . be said . . . to begin here.[7]

Chesterton says that men like Francis "are not common in
any age, nor are they to be fully understood merely by the
exercise of common sense." [8] But, what Francis did by way
of imitating Christ and having others join him in that effort
was common sense. The spectacle of a ragged young man
begging for his building materials as well as begging for his
bread does not sound "progressive" or "practical" at all. In
fact, it seems a very dubious enterprise. What were the practical and progressive results of changing clothes with a beggar? How could such a simple act have any real effect on the
world? The fact is, Francis was able to bring about reform in
the Church without a revolution. The reforms may have
seemed drastic, but they were actually practical, because they
touched something common in men of faith.

   He got hold of the rough brown tunic of a peasant . . . he
   picked up a rope more or less at random . . . and tied it round
   his waist. . . . Ten years later that make-shift costume was the
   uniform of five thousand men; and a hundred years later, in
   that, for a pontifical panoply, they laid the great Dante in the
   grave.[9]

To St. Francis of Assisi, religion was not a thing like a theory,
but a thing like a love affair. He was a romantic. He was a

[7] Ibid., 57–61.
[8] Ibid., 63–64.
[9] Ibid., 65–66.

lover. A lover of God. And really and truly a lover of all men. And a lover of creation. He was a troubadour, and he spoke the true language of the troubadour when he said that he had taken a most glorious and gracious lady and that her name was poverty.

Beyond being a troubadour, he was a jester, a clown of God. He was at once someone who was earnest and solemn and someone who provided comic relief. He knew how to be a fool. A fool for Christ.

He became that fool for Christ after a period of solitude and literal darkness. He entered a cave to be alone with God. Chesterton says that

> the man who went into the cave was not the man who came out again.[10]

He emerged into the light ... with a lightness, the lightness of humility. And he saw the world in a completely different light. In fact, he saw the world upside down.

> If a man saw the world upside down, with all the trees and towers hanging head downwards as in a pool, one effect would be to emphasize the idea *of dependence*.... He would be thankful to God for not dropping the whole cosmos like a vast crystal to be shattered into falling stars. Perhaps St. Peter saw the world so, when he was crucified head-downwards....
>
> In a ... cynical sense ... men have said, "Blessed is he that expecteth nothing, for he shall not be disappointed." It was in a wholly happy and enthusiastic sense that St. Francis said, "Blessed is he who expecteth nothing, for he shall enjoy everything." It was by this deliberate idea of starting from zero

[10] Ibid., 70.

... that he did come to enjoy even earthly things as few people have enjoyed them.[11]

The mystic who passes through the moment when there is nothing but God does in some sense behold the beginning-less beginnings in which there was really nothing else. He not only appreciates everything but the nothing of which everything was made....

This sense of the great gratitude and the sublime dependence ... is ... not a fancy but a fact.... We all depend in every detail ... upon God....

Rosetti makes the remark ... that the worst moment for the atheist is when he is really thankful and has nobody to thank. The converse of this proposition is also true.... All goods look better when they look like gifts....

It may seem a paradox to say that a man may be transported with joy to discover that he is in debt. But this is only because in commercial cases the creditor does not generally share the transports of joy.... But here the word is really the key ... of asceticism. It is the highest and holiest of the paradoxes that the man who really knows he cannot pay his debt will be for ever paying it. He will be for ever giving back what he cannot ... be expected to give back. He will be always throwing things away into a bottomless pit of un-fathomable thanks.[12]

The modern world tends to think of asceticism as something terribly gloomy. Not so, says Chesterton. In fact, if there is one point that he tries to make about Francis it is that he was an ascetic, but he was not gloomy. He was the court jester who grasped the truth of this riddle: "that the whole world

[11] Ibid., 72–73.
[12] Ibid., 74–77.

has only one good thing: a bad debt",[13] As soon as Francis had his vision in which he saw our total dependence on divine love:

> He flung himself into fasting and vigil exactly as he had flung himself furiously into battle.[14]

> He devoured fasting as a man devours food. He plunged after poverty as men have dug madly for gold.[15]

This, says Chesterton, is the great challenge to the modern mind in the whole problem of the pursuit of pleasure. It is an undeniable historical fact that Francis, who instead of spending his life pursuing pleasure, spent his life proving that he was and had nothing, was a happy man. "He was a poet whose whole life was a poem".[16] In fact, he was perhaps the one happy poet among all the unhappy poets of the world. He made the very act of living an art, but unpretentious, unpremeditated, and unrehearsed.

St. Francis also had a "perpetual preoccupation with the idea of brotherhood".[17] Not a back-slapping sort of brotherhood, but a brotherhood actually founded on courtesy.

> He honoured all men; that is, he not only loved them but respected them all.

He saw "the image of God multiplied but never monotonous." There was never a man who looked into Francis' eyes without being certain that Francis was truly interested in him. He was a genuine democrat, in the true meaning of the word.

---

[13] Ibid., 77.
[14] Ibid.
[15] Ibid., 78.
[16] Ibid., 83.
[17] Ibid., 87.

He treated the whole mob of men as a mob of kings.[18]

Of course, Francis is famous for the kinship he felt not only with every person, but also with every fellow creature. His love of nature, however, is perhaps the most misunderstood thing about him. He did not worship nature, which, as Chesterton points out, is an unnatural thing to do. He worshipped the Creator. His love for God was expressed in the charity he showed to God's workmanship. Francis was able to see each tree as a separate and sacred thing, a brother of man and a child of God.

> He did not call nature his mother; he called a particular donkey his brother or a particular sparrow his sister.... That is where his mysticism is so close to the common sense of the child. A child has no difficulty about understanding that God made the dog and the cat; though he is well aware that the making of dogs and cats out of nothing is a mysterious process.... But no child would understand what you meant if you mixed up the dog and the cat and everything else into one monster with a myriad legs and called it nature.[19]

His attitude toward the created world, as toward everything else, was indeed mystical. Chesterton says:

> St. Francis was a mystic, but he believed in mysticism and not in mystification.

He was the mortal enemy of all our modern mystics who "melt away the edges of things" and dissolve everything into everything else. His vision was very clear, very distinct.

[18] Ibid., 88–89.
[19] Ibid., 82.

He was a mystic of the daylight and the darkness; but not a
mystic of the twilight.[20]

But he was not just a mystic. He was a builder as well. Francis went with eleven companions in peasant costume to ask
Pope Innocent III to create a new religious order. Monastic
orders had already been approved by the Church. It was clearly
understood that vows of celibacy and poverty free a person
for a life devoted to prayer and service. Francis, however, did
not call his little brothers monks, but friars. A friar is not
only freer than an ordinary man, he is freer than a monk. It
was important that he should be free from the world, but it
was also necessary that he should be free from the cloister.

> The whole point of a monk was that his economic affairs
> were settled for good; he knew where he would get his sup-
> per, though it was a very plain supper. But the whole point
> of a friar was that he did not know where he would get his
> supper. There was always a possibility that he might get no
> supper.[21]

> There was nothing that the world could hold them by; for
> the world catches us mostly by the fringes of our garments,
> the futile externals of our lives. . . . We may already get a
> glimpse also of the practical side of that asceticism which
> puzzles those who think themselves practical. . . . You could
> not . . . ruin him and threaten to starve a man who was ever
> striving to fast. You could not ruin him and reduce him to
> beggary, for he was already a beggar.[22]

The Church had to look closely at what Francis was pro-
posing. The Church is always on the watch against excessive

---

[20] Ibid.
[21] Ibid., 97.
[22] Ibid., 94.

asceticism and its potential evils. But, says Chesterton, the Vatican decided that while these Franciscans might have a hard life, it was a life "described as ideal in the Gospel." [23]

Now many of the followers of St. Francis treated him as the founder of a religion. As Chesterton says:

> The coming of St. Francis was like the birth of a child in a dark house, lifting its doom.[24]

The Franciscan spirit brought a certain freshness to all the world, and a freshness to the Church as well. For the Church at this time was over a thousand years old and was feeling its age. The freshness and freedom of the first Christians seemed as lost and far away then as it does now. The Church certainly needed the renewal that Francis brought, but there was a real danger that the movement of Francis would sweep up all of Christendom. The Pope understood that as great as Francis was, it was not necessary that every Christian should become like Francis. The Pope rightly determined that the Franciscans would have a specific role within the Church but would not take over the whole Church. Chesterton says that if the Franciscan movement had turned into a new religion, it would have been a narrow religion, something less than the Universal Church.[25]

As for Francis himself, he may have seemed wild and romantic, but he always hung on to reason. He never lost his balance, says Chesterton, because he never lost his sense of humor.[26]

[23] Ibid., 98.
[24] Ibid., 129.
[25] Ibid., 130.
[26] Ibid., 131.

He was always in the light, the light of Christ. He was a mirror of Christ as the moon is a mirror of the sun.[27] He was the mirror of Christ because he was truly an imitator of Christ. He was most inspired by that part of Christ that the rest of us most avoid: his suffering. Chesterton says Francis was full of the sentiment that he had not suffered enough to be worthy even to be a distant follower of his suffering God. He did not feel he was "worthy even of the shadow of the crown of thorns".[28] But he apparently *was* worthy. Francis, the mirror of Christ, even bore on his body the wounds of Christ.

He was a man who suffered but who was endlessly cheerful. A soldier, but a man of peace. A builder, but a beggar. A wise man, but a fool for Christ. A mystic, but a man of action. How do we sum him up? Chesterton says that Francis was above all a great giver. But,

> He cared chiefly for the best kind of giving which is called thanksgiving.

He understood the theory of thanks and knew that

> Its depths are a bottomless abyss. He knew that the praise of God stands on its strongest ground when it stands on nothing.[29]

[27] Ibid., 104.
[28] Ibid., 108.
[29] Ibid., 132.

9

St. Thomas Aquinas

To this question "Is there anything?" St. Thomas begins by answering "Yes"; if he began by answering "No", it would not be the beginning, but the end. That is what some of us call common sense.

— St. Thomas Aquinas.

When G. K. Chesterton was commissioned to write a book about St. Thomas Aquinas, even his strongest supporters and greatest admirers were a little worried. But they would have been a lot *more* worried if they had known how he actually wrote the book.

Chesterton had already written acclaimed studies of Robert Browning, William Blake, Charles Dickens, Robert Louis Stevenson, Chaucer, and St. Francis of Assisi. Nonetheless, there was a great deal of anxiety even among Chesterton's admirers when in 1933 he agreed to take on the Angelic Doctor of the Church, the author of the *Summa Theologica*, St. Thomas Aquinas.

Without consulting any texts whatsoever, Chesterton rapidly dictated about half the book to his secretary, Dorothy

Collins. Then he suddenly said to her, "I want you to go to London and get me some books."

"What books?" asked Dorothy.

"*I* don't know", said G. K.

So Dorothy did some research and brought back a stack of books on St. Thomas. G.K. flipped through a couple of books in the stack, took a walk in his garden, and then, without ever referring to the books again, proceeded to dictate the rest of his book to Dorothy.

Many years later, when Evelyn Waugh heard this story, he quipped that Chesterton never even read the *Summa Theologica*, but merely ran his fingers across the binding and absorbed everything in it. But, of course, Chesterton had read at least parts of the *Summa*. What is amazing is that he read it long before he became a Catholic and thirty years before writing his book on St. Thomas Aquinas.

And what kind of book did he write? Étienne Gilson, probably the most highly respected scholar of St. Thomas in the twentieth century, a man who devoted his whole life to studying St. Thomas, had this to say about Chesterton's book:

> I consider it as being without possible comparison the best book ever written on St. Thomas. Nothing short of genius can account for such an achievement. Everybody will no doubt admit that it is a "clever" book, but the few readers who have spent twenty or thirty years in studying St. Thomas, and who, perhaps, have themselves published two or three volumes on the subject, cannot fail to perceive that the so-called "wit" of Chesterton has put their scholarship to shame. He has guessed all that which they had tried to demonstrate, and he has said everything that they were more or less clumsily attempting to express in academic formulas. Chesterton was one of the deepest thinkers who ever ex-

isted; he was deep because he was right; and he could not help being right; but he could not either help being modest and charitable, so he left it to those who could understand him to know that he was right, and deep; to the others, he apologized for being right, and he made up for being deep by being witty. And that is all they can see of him.[1]

A man as modest as Chesterton is the first to admit that it is difficult to popularize a medieval philosopher. But the fault is not with the medieval philosopher. It is with us and our times. We are no longer very sophisticated thinkers or very precise thinkers. We deal in moods and emotions, especially in the arts, and we have developed a very loose vocabulary along with our loose thinking.

Chesterton also admits that not all of St. Thomas' writings are straightforward and easy to understand. The point is, once you have taken the trouble to understand them, they are very easy to accept. This, he says, is because "Aquinas is almost always on the side of simplicity, and supports the ordinary man's acceptance of ordinary truisms.... His conclusion is what is called the conclusion of common sense; it is his purpose to justify common sense"[2] to those who have rejected it. Aquinas proved he could suffer fools gladly. But with the *Summa*, he proved he could also suffer clever people gladly.[3]

And so Chesterton paints a picture of Aquinas as the Saint of Common Sense, a philosopher who used reason reasonably.

[1] Maisie Ward, *Gilbert Keith Chesterton* (New York: Sheed and Ward, 1942), 620.

[2] *St. Thomas Aquinas*, *CW* 2:517.

[3] Ibid., 514.

He begins by comparing St. Thomas of Aquino with St. Francis of Assisi. There are the obvious contrasts in their appearances, in their style, in fact, in just about everything. But in spite of that, Chesterton says,

> They were really doing the same thing. One of them was doing it in the world of the mind and the other in the world of the worldly.[4]

They "were doing the same great work; one in the study and the other in the street".[5] Neither of them brought anything new to Christianity. Rather, they brought Christianity closer to the kingdom of God. In the process, each of them "reaffirmed the Incarnation, by bringing God back to earth".[6] More than that, they both strengthened what Chesterton calls the "staggering doctrine of the Incarnation". It is the strict interpretation of this doctrine that distinguishes Catholicism not just from all heresies but from all other religions. Chesterton says:

> There cannot be a stiffer piece of Christian divinity than the divinity of Christ.[7]

> As compared with a Jew, a Moslem, a Buddhist, a Deist, or most obvious alternatives, a Christian *means* a man who believes that deity or sanctity has attached to matter or entered the world of the senses. Some modern writers, missing this simple point, have even talked as if the acceptance of Aristotle was a sort of concession to the Arabs.... The Crusaders wanted to recover the place where the body of

[4] Ibid., 426.
[5] Ibid., 428.
[6] Ibid.
[7] Ibid., 433.

Christ had been, because they believed ... that it was a Christian place. St. Thomas wanted to recover what was in essence the body of Christ itself; the sanctified body of the Son of Man which had become a miraculous medium between heaven and earth.... St. Thomas was, if you will, taking the lower road when he walked in the steps of Aristotle. So was God, when He worked in the workshop of Joseph.[8]

St. Thomas was not only intent on upholding the *reality* of the Incarnation. He also wanted to show what were the *implications* of the Incarnation. Bringing heaven and earth together means bringing body and soul together. It means man is to be studied in his whole manhood. A man is not a man without his body, just as a man is not a man without his soul.

A corpse is not a man; but also a ghost is not a man.[9]

St. Thomas stood up stoutly for the fact that a man's body is his body as his mind is his mind; and that *he* can only be a balance and union of the two.[10]

In rejecting the Christian dogma, modernism, in a sense, rejects both body and mind. It rejects the body when it rejects "that most startling sort of dogma ... the Resurrection of the Body".[11] It rejects the mind when it rejects free will, or the moral responsibility of man. Chesterton says:

Upon this sublime and perilous liberty hang heaven and hell, and all the mysterious drama of the soul.[12]

[8] Ibid., 437.
[9] Ibid., 433.
[10] Ibid., 434.
[11] Ibid.
[12] Ibid., 435.

As was said earlier, almost every heresy is against some aspect of the doctrine of the Incarnation. The specific heresy that St. Thomas battled was that of the Manichees, who thought the material world was evil and only the spiritual world was good. But Manicheism is only a variation of other heresies both before and after it: the Gnostics, the Docetists, the Flagellants, the Puritans, the Christian Scientists all share a kind of mystical loathing for physical reality.

St. Thomas is the champion of God the Creator. He affirms what Scripture says, that God created the physical world and all that is in it and said that it was *good*. As a matter of fact, says Chesterton, "the work of heaven alone was material; the making of a material world," and there was nothing evil about it. "The work of hell", on the other hand, "is entirely spiritual." [13] Hell does not create anything. It only destroys.

The modern interpretation of history is that in the period of the "Dark" Ages (A.D. 476–800) and the Middle Ages (800–1400), there was a great philosophical break created by the Catholic Church, a break between the classical thinkers of Greece and Rome and the "Enlightenment" thinkers of the Reformation and the Renaissance. But Chesterton argues that it was St. Thomas who reconnected with the ancient classical philosophers such as Aristotle and that the break in philosophical history came after St. Thomas. And since that time, says Chesterton, there has been nothing but a continued breakdown in philosophy. [14] Most modern philosophies are not philosophy, but philosophic doubt. Most modern thinkers have abandoned that ancient and "unusual human hobby; the habit of thinking". [15]

[13] Ibid., 485.
[14] Ibid., 465.
[15] Ibid.

Chesterton shows how St. Thomas was able to use Aristotle and the so-called "natural" philosophers because he knew that nothing discovered in nature could ultimately contradict the faith. The faith was the one truth, and so, conversely:

Nothing really deduced from the Faith could ultimately contradict the facts.[16]

Faith does not contradict reason. Reason does not contradict faith. And both are necessary. St. Thomas justifies both faith and reason against those who would reduce man's knowledge to one or the other.

Ironically, those who attack the faith in the name of reason invariably end up attacking reason. Skepticism and the philosophies of doubt begin by doubting revelation and end up doubting everything else, including reality.

St. Thomas affirms a fundamental and unmistakable reality. As Chesterton says it so perfectly: "There *is* an Is." [17]

The philosophy of St. Thomas stands founded on the universal common conviction that eggs are eggs. The Hegelian may say that an egg is really a hen, because it is a part of an endless process of Becoming; the Berkeleian may hold that poached eggs only exist as a dream exists; since it is quite as easy to call the dream the cause of the eggs as the eggs the cause of the dream; the Pragmatist may believe that we get the best out of scrambled eggs by forgetting that they ever were eggs, and only remembering the scramble. But no pupil of St. Thomas needs to addle his brains in order adequately to addle his eggs; to put his head at any peculiar angle in looking at eggs, or squinting at eggs, or winking the other eye in order to see a new simplification of eggs. The

[16] Ibid., 475.
[17] Ibid., 529.

Thomist stands in the broad daylight of the brotherhood of
men, in their common consciousness that eggs are not hens
or dreams or mere practical assumptions; but things attested
by the Authority of the Senses, which is from God.[18]

Our senses are doors and windows that open up on a world
that really is there. But then comes the next step in this philosophy of common sense. We know that what we see is
really there, that our senses do not deceive us, but we also
know that there is also more to what we see than what we
see. We know we do not see the whole picture. St. Thomas'
reasoning is this: Since what we see is incomplete or imper-
fect, that means there is something that *is* complete and *is*
perfect. Modern philosophers take this incompleteness and
imperfection and go the other direction with it. They use
the incompleteness they know to conclude that there is no
completeness anywhere, that everything is merely scattered
and adrift and in a state of flux. But this type of reasoning
quickly crumbles. It means that nothing can even be itself. It
means there is no ideal, no perfection. It means we cannot
ever say a change is for the better—because there is no best.
But the Christian philosophy identifies Completion and Perfection. It is God. Anyone who thinks about it long enough
realizes that Christianity provides not only the only permanent philosophy, but the only working philosophy.

Of nearly all other philosophies it is strictly true that their
followers work in spite of them, or do not work at all. No
sceptics work sceptically; no fatalists work fatalistically; all
without exception work on the principle that it is possible
to assume what it is not possible to believe. No materialist

who thinks his mind was made up for him, by mud and blood and heredity, has any hesitation in making up his mind. No sceptic who believes that truth is subjective has any hesitation about treating it as objective.[19]

In other words, what the other philosophies lack is common sense.

Chesterton says that since the sixteenth century, nobody's system of philosophy has really corresponded to everybody's sense of reality. Each of them asks us to believe something that no normal man would believe: "that law is above right, or right is outside reason, or things are only as we think them, or everything is relative to a reality that is not there."[20] The modern philosopher claims, "like a sort of confidence man",[21] that if once we will grant him this, the rest will be easy, that if at one point we just sacrifice our sanity, everything else will make sense.

But the point is, none of the modern philosophies makes any sense to the man on the street. Surprisingly, the philosophy that is closest to the mind of the man on the street is the philosophy of St. Thomas Aquinas. It is firmly rooted in reality, fully respectful of human dignity, and, in every sense of the word, reasonable.

Now, reason may lead you to the truth, but it cannot make you drink. This is where free will enters the picture. It is still up to you to make a decision about the truth, because the decision is going to change your life.

Modern skeptics have tried to avoid the decision by obscuring the truth, by saying truth is relative. By saying there

[19] Ibid., 542–43.
[20] Ibid., 514.
[21] Ibid.

is not one truth. By saying it does not matter what you be
lieve. Even if you believe a lie.

> There is a false and true ... the division and dilemma that
> brings the ultimate sort of war into the world; the everlast-
> ing duel between Yes and No. This is the dilemma that many
> sceptics have darkened the universe and dissolved the mind,
> solely in order to escape. They are those who maintain that
> there is something that is both Yes and No. I do not know
> whether they pronounce it Yo.[22]

One final point. By being the champion of God the Creator
against the heresy of the Manichees, who considered the physical world evil, St. Thomas was ultimately defending God's
most precious and mysterious creation: life. Above all else,
St. Thomas believed in life. And life is exactly what is doubted
most in today's culture of death. We are living the legacy of
what Chesterton calls "the morbid Renaissance intellectual"
who says, "To be or not to be—that is the question." But St.
Thomas Aquinas, says Chesterton, replies in a voice of thun-
der, "To be—that is the answer." [23]

As we noted earlier Chesterton begins this book by discussing the differences between the two friars, Francis of Assisi and Thomas Aquinas. And the point of their differences
is this: When the world forgot romance, it discovered St.
Francis. When it forgot reason, it discovered St. Thomas Aquinas. The Church always has exactly what the world is lacking. It is of course a testament to the greatness and universality
of the Church that it has saints as different as Francis and
Thomas. But I would like to add that it is a testament to the

[22] Ibid., 529.
[23] Ibid., 489.

greatness of G. K. Chesterton that he could write with such understanding and clarity about two such different saints. He matched the mind of Aquinas with the soul of Francis. He was concerned with truth as clearly as it could be articulated. He was concerned with justice and charity as plainly as they could be embodied. At the beginning of this book on St. Thomas, he pictures the two saints, Francis and Thomas—who lived a hundred years apart—walking down the road together. I like to picture G. K. Chesterton walking between them.

10

The Everlasting Man

A mass of legend and literature ... has repeated and rung
the changes on that single paradox; that the hands that
had made the sun and stars were too small to reach the
huge heads of the cattle. Upon this paradox, ... all the
literature of our faith is founded ... something that would
be much too good to be true, except that it is true.

— *The Everlasting Man*

Chesterton's book *The Everlasting Man* was written in 1925,
and it is certainly one of his most important works. C. S.
Lewis called it the best book of Christian apologetics that he
had ever read.[1] In fact, Lewis was an atheist before he read
the book, but not afterward. And yet *The Everlasting Man* is
not really a book of apologetics at all. It is a sweeping history
of the world. The fact that it also provides a well-reasoned
defense of Christianity is only because Chesterton clearly
shows who is the central figure in all of history.

He begins by explaining that the critics of Christianity
offer no real perspective from which they fling their doubts.

---

[1] Quoted in Sheldon Vanauken, *A Severe Mercy* (San Francisco: Harper and
Row, 1977), 90.

"Their criticism", he says, "has taken on a curious tone; as of a random and illiterate heckling." [2] They will complain and explain that churches are empty "without even going there to find out if they are empty, or which of them are empty".[3] They will condemn the Church for condemning sin and then turn around and claim that since the world has become so evil and hopeless, it proves that the Church is wrong.

> When the world goes wrong, it proves rather that the Church is right. The Church is justified, not because her children do not sin, but because they do.[4]

Chesterton says that the main problem with the critics of the Church is that they are too close to it to see it. They cannot see the big picture, only the small picture that may affect them. With their sulks and their perversity and their petty criticism, they are merely reacting to the Church. They are too close; they are not able to see it for what it really is. What they need to do is back up. The purpose of *The Everlasting Man* is to get the reader to back up far enough to see The Thing, the Christian faith, from truly an objective viewpoint. Then he might see that The Thing is what it claims to be.

> It is exactly when the boy gets far enough off to see the giant that he sees that he really is a giant. It is exactly when we do at last see the Christian Church afar ... that we see that it is really the Church of Christ.[5]

[2] *The Everlasting Man, CW* 2:143.
[3] Ibid., 144.
[4] Ibid.
[5] Ibid., 146.

The book was written as a kind of rebuttal to H. G. Wells' popular book *The Outline of History*. You would think that such an outline would feature the most outstanding events and figures in history, but Wells completely glossed over the two biggest points. The first is the creature called man, and the second is the man called Christ. Any honest student of history will admit that man stands apart from all the other creatures and that Christ stands apart from all other men. But Wells tried to treat man as just another animal and Christ as just another man. Unfortunately, most modern historians have followed Wells' lead.

So Chesterton begins with the man in the cave. Literally. The caveman. The Darwinians see this figure as a descendent of apelike beasts, with the caveman being little more than an ape himself. But Chesterton argues that Darwin's theory about the origin of man has not been proven, even though it is treated as if it were. It has even been turned into an article of faith. Yet not only is it based on scant evidence: elaborate reconstructions based on bits of bone and teeth. Even then Chesterton noted that if we dare to question such evidence we will be faced with fierce ridicule.

> Sometimes the professor with his bone becomes almost as dangerous as a dog with his bone.... They talk of searching for the habits and habitat of the Missing Link; as if one were to talk of being on friendly terms with the gap in a narrative or the hole in an argument, of taking a walk with a *non-sequitur* or dining with an undistributed middle.[6]

Chesterton insists that the origin of the universe, the origin of life, and the origin of man are things shrouded in mystery.

[6] Ibid., 173–74.

We cannot possibly imagine how the world was created any more than we could create one.

> Evolution really is mistaken for explanation. It has the fatal quality of leaving on many minds the impression that they do understand it and everything else; just as many of them live under a sort of illusion that they have read the *Origin of Species*.[7]

So what do we know about the man in the cave? The one thing we really do know about the caveman is that he was an artist. He left behind his drawings on the wall of the cave, where they are still available for viewing. The creature who made these drawings was truly different from all other creatures; because he was a creator as well as a creature. Says Chesterton: "Art is the signature of man."[8] It is just one of many things that demonstrates that:

> The more we really look at man as an animal, the less he will look like one.[9]

> The simplest truth about man is that he is a very strange being; almost in the sense of being a stranger on the earth. . . . He has much more of the external appearance of one bringing alien habits from another land than of a mere growth of this one. He has an unfair advantage and an unfair disadvantage. He cannot sleep in his own skin; he cannot trust his own instincts. He is at once a creator moving miraculous hands and fingers and a kind of cripple. He is wrapped in artificial bandages called clothes; he is propped on artificial crutches called furniture. His mind has the same doubtful liberties and the same wild limitations. Alone among the

[7] Ibid., 156.
[8] Ibid., 166.
[9] Ibid., 159.

animals, he is shaken with the beautiful madness called laughter.... Alone among the animals he feels ... the mystery of shame. Whether we praise these things as natural to man or abuse them as artificial in nature, they remain in the same sense unique. This is realised by the whole popular instinct called religion.[10]

Those who try to explain religion only try to explain it away. They try to use our longing for God as evidence that there is no God. As if hunger were evidence that there is no such thing as food.

Religion is as old as civilization. And civilization is as old as history. Chesterton says that when we study history, the curtain rises on a play already in progress.[11] He argues that it was religion that advanced civilization. It was religion that dealt with the meanings of things, with the development and interpretation of symbols, which advanced communication and knowledge, or what we call the arts and the sciences.

A politician once told me in a debate that I was resisting modern reforms exactly as some ancient priest probably resisted the discovery of wheels. I pointed out, in reply, that it was far more likely that the ancient priest made the discovery of the wheels. It is overwhelmingly probable that the ancient priest had a great deal to do with the discovery of the art of writing.[12]

Chesterton speculates that most ancient tribes were initially monotheistic, that is, they believed in only one God. But as tribes combined in larger cities, they combined their gods as well. There was, of course, one notable exception. The Jews.

[10] Ibid., 168.
[11] Ibid., 193.
[12] Ibid., 199.

Other historians try to paint the Jewish God as something narrow. Chesterton says this God turned out to be only as narrow as the universe. The Jews protected and preserved the greatest truth of ancient times. "The world", he says, "owes God to the Jews." [13]

The religions of most other ancient peoples were less about theology than about mythology. Their heavens became populated with gods as frail as themselves. Mythology is about the imagination, that is, it is about images that fill the mind. Chesterton says they are infinitely suggestive, and we all know what they suggest ... until some scholar tells us. [14] We know that the myths are stories about an ache for the eternal, especially an ache for eternal life. The ancient myths may be heroic, but they are ultimately hopeless. Orpheus cannot quite bring back Eurydice from the dead. The myths are not able to answer the riddles they raise. And when people realize their hopelessness, their society begins to collapse.

If we study any civilization, we see that after progress comes decay. Chesterton says men do not grow tired of evil but of good. [15] They become weary of joy. They stop worshipping God and start worshipping idols, their own bad imitations of God, and they become as wooden as the thing they worship. They start worshipping nature and become unnatural. They start worshipping sex and become perverted. Men start lusting after men and become unmanly.

> The most ignorant of humanity know by the very look of earth that they have forgotten heaven. [16]

[13] Ibid., 227.
[14] Ibid., 243.
[15] Ibid., 285.
[16] Ibid., 226.

But then something marvelous happens in history. And it also happens in a cave. A cave in Bethlehem.

Chesterton calls Bethlehem a place where extremes meet. It is where heaven meets earth. God comes to make a home in the world and finds himself homeless. And religion and philosophy come together for the first time. The kings and shepherds kneel down together before a manger in Bethlehem. Men of different lands, different cultures, different tastes and educations and aspirations all find what they are looking for in the same thing. The shepherds find their Shepherd, and the kings find their King.

The coming of the man called Christ changes everything. It is a story like none other. We have forgotten how unique, how strange and startling it really is.

Remember, the purpose of this book, *The Everlasting Man*, is to get us to look at the claims of the Christian faith as a true outsider might. Chesterton says that if we approach the Gospel objectively we will see that it is not a book of platitudes. It paints a picture of a man who was indeed a wonderworker, but who spoke in riddles and rebukes. His teachings were as difficult to accept in his own time as they are today. None of the critics of Christianity seem to appreciate the fact that Christ's teachings were not dependent on the social order in which he lived but transcended their time altogether.

> The truth is that when critics have spoken of the local limitations of the Galilean, it has always been a case of the local limitations of the critics.[17]

The critics of course try to create a different Christ from the one portrayed in the Gospels by picking and choosing whatever they want. They always try to make him merely hu-

[17] Ibid., 327.

man, whether they make him a socialist or a pacifist or a madman. Chesterton says:

> There must surely have been something not only mysterious but many-sided about Christ if so many smaller Christs can be carved out of him.[18]

But the main impression one gets from studying the teachings of Christ is that he really did not come to teach. What separates Christianity from other religions is that its central figure does not wish to be known merely as a teacher. He makes the greatest claim of all. Muhammad did not claim to be God. Buddha did not claim to be God. Christ did claim to be God.

The story gets stranger still. It is indeed as Chesterton calls it, "The Strangest Story in the World".[19] All of Christ's life is a steady pursuit of the ultimate sacrifice. The Gospel tells the story in plain words.

> Every attempt to amplify that story has diminished it.[20]

As Jesus is murdered, he prays for all the murderous race of men and asks that they be forgiven, for "they know not what they do."

> All the great groups that stood about the Cross represent in one way or another the great historical truth of the time; that the world could not save itself. Man could do no more. Rome and Jerusalem and Athens and everything else were going down like a sea turned into a slow cataract.... The strength of the world ... was turned to weakness and the wisdom of the world ... was turned to folly.[21]

[18] Ibid., 329.
[19] Ibid., 331.
[20] Ibid., 340.
[21] Ibid., 341–42.

The wisdom of the world was turned to folly because who would have thought that the local execution of a minor revolutionary in an obscure outpost would become the central event in all of history. But that is where the Cross stands: at the center of history. And Chesterton does not miss the opportunity to make one of his great puns:

The cross is the crux of the whole matter.[22]

This central dogma of the Christian faith, that God died, that, as Chesterton says, God was for one instant forsaken of God,[23] that God sacrificed himself to himself, is more mysterious than anything, even the mystery of creation itself. Those who object to this dogma do so not because the dogma is bad, but because it is too good to be true. What they really reject is the freedom that fills the Christian creed. They reject the dogma that gives man so much freedom as to allow him to fall. They reject the dogma that gives God so much freedom as to allow him to die. They reject the dogma as the truth, because the truth would set them free.

But the Gospel story does not end with God's death; it ends with the most startling episode of all. An empty grave. And God again walking in a garden, as on the first day of creation. The Gospel story ends, not with an ending, but with a beginning. It is the beginning of the Church.

Chesterton makes the all-important point that Christianity appeared as a Church, "with everything that is implied in a Church and much that is disliked in a Church".[24] It did not begin as an ethical movement or a school of idealists; it began as a Church. It had a doctrine and a discipline. It had

[22] Ibid., 266.
[23] Ibid., 344.
[24] Ibid., 349.

sacraments and rituals. It admitted people and expelled people. It affirmed dogma with authority and rejected false teaching the same way. And he says that Christianity satisfied our fundamental human longings by doing what no other religion had ever done:

> It met the mythological search for romance by being a story and the philosophical search for truth by being a true story.[25]

The more we study it, the more we see that Christianity is truly different from any other religion, just as man is truly different from any other creature. The Church carried a unique message, and it puzzled the world that its members acted like messengers. They even called their message the gospel, the good news. But, as Chesterton says, "Nobody else except those messengers has any Gospel; nobody else has any good news; for the simple reason that nobody else has any news" at all.[26]

> The creed was like a key.... First, a key is above all things a thing with a shape. It is a thing that depends entirely upon keeping its shape. The Christian creed is above all things the philosophy of shapes and the enemy of shapelessness.... It differs from all that formless infinity ... which makes a sort of pool of night in the dark heart of Asia.... It differs also from the ... vagueness of mere evolutionism, the idea of creatures constantly losing their shape. A man told that his solitary latchkey had been melted down with a million others into a Buddhistic unity would be annoyed. But a man told that his key was gradually growing and sprouting in his pocket, and branching into new ... complications, would not be more gratified.

[25] Ibid., 380.
[26] Ibid., 401.

Second, the shape of a key is ... a rather fantastic shape ... [and] arbitrary.... A key is not a matter of argument. It either fits the lock or it does not. It is useless for men to stand disputing over it ... or reconstructing it on pure principles of geometry or decorative art. It is senseless for a man to say he would like a simpler key; it would be far more sensible to do his best with a crowbar. And thirdly, ... the key is necessarily a thing with a pattern ... a rather elaborate pattern. When people complain of the religion being so ... complicated with theology and things of the kind, they forget that the world [is complicated.]... It was also full of secrets, of unexplored and unfathomable fallacies, of unconscious mental diseases, of dangers in all directions. If the faith had faced the world only with platitudes about peace and simplicity ..., it would not have had the faintest effect on that luxurious and labyrinthine lunatic asylum.... There was undoubtedly much about the key that seemed complex; indeed there was only one thing about it that was simple. It opened the door.[27]

We sometimes hear it said that Christianity shook the world. But Chesterton says that Christianity "did not shake the world; it steadied the world".[28]

It has endured for nearly two thousand years; and the world within it has been more lucid, more level-headed, more reasonable in its hopes, more healthy in its instincts, more humorous and cheerful in the face of fate and death, than all the world outside.[29]

The soul of Christendom, he says, is common sense.

Christianity has done something different from just surviving. It has defeated its enemies by following the example

[27] Ibid., 346–47.
[28] Ibid., 401.
[29] Ibid., 402.

of Christ. Not just by saying the right thing and doing the right thing, not by marvels and not by might, but by resurrection, by returning to life after having been apparently defeated. As Chesterton says:

> Christianity has died many times and risen again; for it had a God who knew the way out of the grave.[30]

[30] Ibid., 382.

11

The Outline of Sanity

I could do a great many things before I came to definitely
anti-social action like robbing a bank or (worse still) working in a bank.

— *The Outline of Sanity*

To save seventy-five cents on a six-month supply of toilet
paper we drive across town to the Discount Super Store,
which is owned by some multinational corporation, while
the corner shop, which is owned by our neighbor, goes out
of business. A defense contractor successfully lobbies congress to build a billion-dollar fighter jet because it would be
technologically superior to the planes the contractor is now
building and selling to our enemies. Movie stars make millions for pretending to be someone else. Farmers are fore-
closed on for trying merely to be themselves. The world is
insane.

Chesterton once said that we must "hate [the world]
enough to want to change it, and yet love it enough to think
it worth changing".[1] When we talk about changing the world,

---

[1] *Orthodoxy, CW* 1:275.

at some point we have to talk about economic issues, about money and machines and our daily bread. Chesterton deals with these in his book *The Outline of Sanity*. It is an "outline" in that it is not a complete or systematic treatment, but a collection of essays from Chesterton's own newspaper, *G. K.'s Weekly*. But while it is only an outline, it *is* sanity. It represents right thinking in a world that has lost its mind along with its soul.

Economics can be an incredibly boring subject, with a lot of technical and obscure terms, which is why, too often, it is left only to economists to discuss while the rest of us ignore them the best we can. One of the problems of the modern world is that in our vague and limited understanding of economics, we think there are only two economic systems to choose from: socialism and capitalism. We have reinforced this limited choice by putting socialism in our left hand and capitalism in our right hand, leaving no other hands. The defenders of socialism tell us that socialism represents security, that all our needs will be taken care of by the government. The defenders of capitalism tell us that capitalism represents freedom, that we are on our own and no one can stop us from going out there and making as much money as we want. What the two systems have in common is that ultimately they are both opposed to the widespread ownership of property. What the socialists do not tell us is that the natural result of their philosophy is that the government ends up owning all property and controlling every aspect of life along with it. And what the capitalists do not tell us is that the natural result of their philosophy is the same result as a game of Monopoly: one person owns everything, and everyone else owns nothing.

What neither of them will tell us is that there is another alternative, a third way, an economic philosophy that is neither

socialism nor capitalism. It offers freedom (which is respon
sibility) and security (which is protection of the individual
and the community). It is based on the widespread ownership of private property. It presumes that small business is
better than big business, that craftsmanship is superior to mass
production, and that local government is better than big government. This economic system goes by the awkward and
misunderstood name of distributism.

The term distributism comes from the phrase "distribu-
tive justice", which was first used by Pope Leo XIII in 1891
in his encyclical *Rerum Novarum*. Pope Leo wrote,

> Among the many and grave duties of rulers who would do
> their best for the people, the first and most important is to
> act with strict justice—with that justice which is called
> distributive—towards each and every class alike.[2]

He says that the wealth of any state "is gained only by the
labor of its working class, therefore justice demands that the
interests of the poorer classes should be carefully watched
over ... so that they who contribute so largely to the advantage of the community may themselves share in the benefits
which they create."[3] Pope Leo says that these people have
the right to be housed, and clothed, and fed.

> Private ownership is sacred and inviolable.... [Public poli-
> cy] should induce as many as possible of the humbler class to
> become owners. Many excellent results will follow from this;
> first of all, property will certainly become more equitably

---

[2] *Rerum Novarum* ("On the Condition of the Working Classes"), *The Great
Encyclical Letters of Pope Leo XII* (Rockford, Ill.: Tan Books, 1995), 228.
[3] Ibid., 229–30.

divided.... Men always work harder and more readily when they work on that which belongs to them.[4]

This visionary Pope recognized the connection between property and justice. G. K. Chesterton, a few decades later in *The Outline of Sanity*, carries this idea forward and shows how neither socialism nor capitalism promotes justice because neither promotes small property.

> A pickpocket is obviously a champion of private enterprise. But it would perhaps be an exaggeration to say that a pickpocket is a champion of private property. The point about Capitalism and Commercialism ... is that they have really preached the extension of business rather than the preservation of belongings; and have at best tried to disguise the pickpocket with some of the virtues of the pirate. The point about Communism is that it only reforms the pickpocket by forbidding pockets.[5]

We are going to consider briefly Chesterton's criticisms of both socialism and capitalism and then his defense of distributism.

Socialism means putting all your eggs in one basket. And then the government takes away the basket. Chesterton says there is not much difference between the present world and socialism except for the fact that the present world leaves out a few ornamental details of socialism, such as justice, citizenship, the elimination of hunger, and so on.[6]

Socialism does not accomplish any of the things it sets out to do because those who hold the socialist philosophy do

[4] Ibid., 237.
[5] *The Outline of Sanity*, CW 5:41.
[6] Ibid., 77–78.

not trust the common man and leave nothing to common sense. Like so many other modern philosophies, socialism is "a new doubt".

> It is not merely a doubt about God; it is rather specially a doubt about Man. The old morality, the Christian religion, the Catholic Church, differed from all this new mentality because it really believed in the rights of men. That is, believed that ordinary men were clothed with powers and privileges and a kind of authority. Thus the ordinary man had ... the right of property ...; a right to judge about his own health, and what risks he would take with the ordinary things of his environment ...; a right to judge of his children's health, and generally to bring up children to the best of his ability.... Now in these primary things in which the old religion trusted a man, the new philosophy utterly distrusts a man.[7]

While Chesterton sees big government as a primary enemy of property and of the very basic freedoms it is supposed to protect, he reserves even stronger words for the pitfalls of capitalism. He says that, ironically, capitalism has done all that socialism threatened to do.[8] Under capitalism, a clerk lives in a house that he does not own, that he did not make, and that he does not want. He thinks in terms of wages, of putting in time. It would make no difference to a clerk of a huge corporation if his job were instead in a government department. It makes no difference if he is a faceless servant of the State or of the rich.

> The capitalist system, good or bad, right or wrong, rests upon two ideas: that the rich will always be rich enough to hire

[7] Ibid., 207–8.
[8] Ibid., 78.

the poor; and the poor will always be poor enough to want to be hired.[9]

Capitalism contradicts itself to the point of paralysis.

> When most men are wage-earners, it is more and more difficult for most men to be customers. For the capitalist is always trying to cut down what his servant demands, and in doing so is cutting down what his customer can spend.[10]

He is wanting the same man to be rich and poor at the same time.

Chesterton prophetically describes "The Bluff of the Big Shops".[11] In 1926, he saw clearly that today's "superstores" would snuff out small local shops, and in almost every way it would be the customer who would suffer. With the elimination of the small shops, there is no more shopping around. At the big shop we really cannot get what we want, only what the big shop wants us to want. We have to deal with clerks who are wage-earners and not owners and who are probably as dissatisfied with the big shop as we are.

> I think the big shop is a bad shop.... Shopping there is not only a bad action but a bad bargain. I think the monster emporium is not only vulgar and insolent, but incompetent and uncomfortable; and I deny that its large organization is efficient. Large organization ... is always disorganization.[12]

> There are far more blunders in a big shop than ever happen in a small shop, where the individual customer can curse the individual shopkeeper. Confronted with modern efficiency

[9] Ibid., 57–58.
[10] Ibid., 59.
[11] Ibid., 85.
[12] Ibid.

the customer is silent; well aware of that organization's talent
for sacking the wrong man....

One of the funniest [claims] is the statement that it is
convenient to get everything in the same shop. That is to
say, it is convenient to walk the length of the street, so long
as you walk indoors or ... underground, instead of walking
the same distance in the open air from one little shop to
another. The truth is that the monopolists' shops are really
very convenient—to the monopolist. They have all the advantage of concentrating business as they concentrate wealth,
in fewer and fewer of the citizens.[13]

We hear a lot of grumbling about big shops, says Chesterton, not because they are big, but because they are bad. And
we know they are bad, even if there is a loud, blaring voice
telling us they are good.

When the millionaire owning the stores is criticized, it is by
his customers. When he is handsomely complimented, it is
by himself ... proclaimed from the house-tops ... [in] a voice
loud enough to drown any remarks made by the public.[14]

There is a word for this. The word is "advertising". Advertising is the voice of the big shop drowning out the voice of
the public.

Chesterton says we do not have to surrender to modern
monopoly. He suggests a very simple counterattack:

One way of supporting small shops would be to support them.
Everybody could do it, but nobody can imagine it being
done. In one sense nothing is so simple, and in another nothing is so hard.[15]

[13] Ibid., 86
[14] Ibid., 203.
[15] Ibid., 110.

And this perhaps is his most important point, one that flies in the face of all other economic theories: Surrendering to the big shops and to monopolies is not a matter of economic law but of moral will.[16]

Chesterton's preferred solution is that most every business be a small business. Where larger businesses may be necessary, they should be owned by the employees; they should be run by a guild, combining their contributions and dividing their results. He believes that small shops can be governed—even if they are self-governed. He believes small shops can be supported—if we support them.

Distributism *is* democracy. Democracy can work only if property is widespread. Distributism is based on property. It is also based on peasantry. Peasantry is another misunderstood and misused word. The simplest way to understand what a peasantry is, is this: self-support, self-control, and self-government.[17] It means people produce and use their own goods, make their own laws, and are dependent on no outsiders. Chesterton says that peasants are "a multitude of men ... standing on their own feet, because they are standing on their own land".[18]

Just as Chesterton used fairy tales in his book *Orthodoxy* to support the basic precepts of Christianity, so he uses fairy tales to support the basic precepts of distributism.

> "Jack and the Beanstalk" ... begins with the strange and startling words, "There once was a poor woman who had a cow.[19]

[16] Ibid., 113.
[17] Ibid., 136.
[18] Ibid., 124.
[19] Ibid., 119.

It would be "a wild paradox" says Chesterton, for the modern world to imagine that a *poor* woman could have a cow. Furthermore, if a poor woman really did have a cow, she would be a true conservative, because she would actually have something to conserve. Many of the people who call themselves conservative are nothing of the sort. The commercial class is the very opposite of conservative, because it is forever using new methods and seeking new markets. And whatever an aristocracy is, it is not conservative. By its very nature it follows fashion and not tradition. Men living a life of leisure and luxury are always depressingly eager for new things. Chesterton argues that if we actually had a peasantry we would have a traditional class, a truly conservative class.[20] The elitist complaint against peasants is that they are dreary and degraded savages. But the reality is that all over the world peasants produce the most beautiful and intricate and uplifting art and that peasant dances are joyful and colorful. They are conservative in a positive sense.

> They conserve customs that do not perish like fashions, and crafts less ephemeral than those artistic movements which so very soon cease to move.... Peasants have produced art because they were communal but not communist. Custom and a corporate tradition gave unity to their art; but each man was a separate artist. It is the ... creative instinct in the individual that makes the peasantry as a whole content and therefore conservative.[21]

The peasant lives, not merely a simple life, but a complete life.[22] Chesterton says the core of a community should be a

---

[20] Ibid., 122.
[21] Ibid., 123–24.
[22] Ibid., 155–56.

body of citizens who go about the business of producing and consuming, not simply exchanging.[23] A society that over-emphasizes trade becomes complex and fragmented, where people have no sense of completeness and certainly no sense of contentment. The modern man in the modern town does not know the cause of things. He does not know where things come from. Chesterton says, he is like the cultivated fellow "who said he liked milk out of a clean shop and not a dirty cow".[24] Safe to say, that man is not living a complete life.

Chesterton does not say there is no place for exchange; nor does he say that man needs nothing from the State. These things must exist, but in proper proportion. Neither the trader nor the government official should play a dominant role in society. He says that at the center of civilization there needs to be a type that is "truly independent; in the sense of producing and consuming within its own social circle".[25]

> There cannot be a nation of millionaires, and there has never yet been a nation of Utopian comrades; but there have been any number of nations of tolerably contented peasants.... The point is that if we do not directly demand the religion of small property, we must at least demand the poetry of small property.... The practical problem is the *goal*....[26]

> The aim of human polity is human happiness.... There is no obligation on us to be richer, or busier, or more efficient, or more productive, or more progressive, or in any way world-lier or wealthier, if it does not make us happier.[27]

[23] Ibid., 140.
[24] Ibid., 137.
[25] Ibid., 140.
[26] Ibid., 192.
[27] Ibid., 145.

It is worth repeating, since we so seldom hear it, that it is possible to be happy without being rich. Happiness can indeed be a hard taskmaster.[28] It tells us not to get entangled with many things. And one of the things with which we have most entangled ourselves is technology. Chesterton says that machines are neither good nor bad, but he does say that becoming dependent on machines can be bad.[29] The point about machines is that we have to be as free not to use them as to use them. Depending on them for our happiness means giving machines the power to make us miserable, which of course they do, as anyone who owns a computer knows.

Chesterton prophetically says that machines have become our religion.[30] We have put our complete faith in them, and they have served to make us more passive and more narrow, less creative and less free. We are no longer pleasure-makers, as peasants are, but pleasure seekers. Machines have created leisure, but we fill even our leisure with machines. Chesterton says we have forgotten the very meaning of the word "manufacture", which is to make things by hand. Our churches, our houses, our furniture, our art all reflect the loss of craftsmanship. Chesterton says we have turned society "into a machine for manufacturing tenth-rate things, and keeping people ignorant of first-rate things".[31]

Big government and big business have used machinery to push us toward consolidation and a rather flat world of standardization. The problem is that big government and big business are both soulless. They are in revolt against the nor-

[28] Ibid., 146.
[29] Ibid., 166.
[30] Ibid., 159.
[31] Ibid., 200.

mal and the ordinary. "They are in revolt against the Citizen." They do not want the common a man to have power.

> They are willing to give him a vote, because they have long discovered that it need not give him any power. They are not willing to give him a house, or a wife, or a child, or a dog, or a cow, or a piece of land, because these things really do give him power.[32]

To combat all this, says Chesterton, we need a moral movement. We have to be able to criticize ourselves. We have to be able to resist the tendencies toward consolidation. We have to resist monopolies. We have to resist endless and invasive bureaucracies. We have to resist the mentality that does not trust the common man to be able take care of himself and his family.

Can it be done? Chesterton says, distributism is a thing done *by* people; it is not a thing that can be done *to* people.[33] It can be done, if we decide to do it. This does not mean that we must all become peasants, that each of us must abandon his career and acquire his proverbial three acres and a cow. But it does mean making some changes. It means making some sacrifices. It means that we take greater control over our economic lives and over our family lives. It means that we actively avoid becoming wage slaves and consumer slaves. It means being fair and being free and being faithful.

Generally I like to give the last word to Chesterton, but the distributist ideal is perhaps best described by another writer, a man who was a shepherd, a soldier, a poet, and a

---

[32] Ibid., 208–9.
[33] Ibid., 201.

king. And like Jack, he was also a giant killer. Like you and me, he was also a sinner. His name was David. And in Psalm 37, (NIV, vv. 3–4, 6) he wrote:

Trust in the LORD, and do good;
 dwell in the land and enjoy safe pasture.
Delight yourself in the LORD
 and he will give you the desires of your heart. . . .
He will make your righteousness shine like the dawn,
 the justice of your cause like the noonday sun.

12

The Superstition of Divorce

> The obvious effect of frivolous divorce will be frivolous
> marriage. If people can be separated for no reason they
> will feel it all the easier to be united for no reason.
>
> — *The Superstition of Divorce*

The family is under attack in our society. We already know
that. But G. K. Chesterton saw the attack coming and saw
where it was coming from.

He wrote *The Superstition of Divorce* in 1920. He said it was
not supposed to be a book, but a pamphlet, and:

> It is the object of a pamphlet to be out of date as soon as
> possible. It can only survive when it does not succeed.[1]

Well, it has survived, which means, as a pamphlet, it did not
succeed. Its arguments are still pertinent; its warnings are
more urgent than ever; its prophecies have unfortunately been
fulfilled.

Chesterton wrote this book two years before he became a
Catholic. Yet, already he is defending the Catholic teaching

---

[1] *The Superstition of Divorce, CW* 4:289.

on marriage. He understands that marriage is not just a contract or a convenience. It is something mystical and elemental. It is part of the very foundation of humanity and connected directly to the divine. In short, it is a sacrament.

As with so many other things, the Church holds strongly to its position on marriage when the rest of the world weakens on it. Chesterton says that:

> The religion that holds it most strongly will hold it when nobody else holds it.[2]

And for him, that is not only an argument in favor of marriage, but also an argument in favor of the Church.

In this book, however, Chesterton purposely does not talk about the sacramental and religious nature of marriage, but rather he focuses on the practical and historical and social reasons for it. He wants to show how the natural reasons for marriage support the supernatural reasons. His main point is that if the family breaks apart, the whole society will break apart.

As far back as 1908 Chesterton noticed an increase in divorce. In a newspaper column he observed that Americans were passing new laws to make divorce easier. Couples were allowed "to get a divorce for incompatibility of temper".[3] He said that if Americans could be divorced for "incompatibility of temper", he could not understand why they were not all divorced. He said that man and woman, as such, are incompatible. The whole aim of marriage is to fight through and survive the incompatibility. He warned that a marriage would be called a failure just because it was a struggle. Just because a man bumps into something, he considers it an ob-

[2] Ibid., 232.
[3] *Illustrated London News*, September 19, 1908, *CW*, 28:180.

stacle and he tries to get rid of it, even if the "obstacle" is the pillar that is holding up the roof of his house.[4]

In *The Superstition of Divorce*, he puts the problem of divorce into its larger context. Divorce, by any account, is a failure. Yet the modern world has begun to portray divorce as a freedom. This comes as no surprise to Chesterton. The modern world, he says, specializes in two forms of freedom: suicide and divorce. In a dreary time we listen to two counsels of despair: the freedom from life and the freedom from love. In our society, he says, where every real freedom has been curtailed, the two doors of death and divorce stand open. But just as we should not accept a system that drives men to drown and shoot themselves, we should not accept a system that produces so many divorces. He insists that we admit that divorce is a failure and that it would be much better for us to find the cause and cure rather than allow divorce to complete its destructive effect.[5]

According to Chesterton, some people say they want divorce in the second place without ever asking themselves if they want marriage in the first place.[6] He suggests we begin with the first question.

What is marriage? Chesterton says it is a promise. More than that, it is a vow. To those who would say that it is a rash vow, his response is that all vows are rash vows,[7] whether they be vows of chivalry or celibacy or matrimony. Freedom means being free to bind oneself, which is what a vow is. A vow, he says, "is a tryst with oneself".[8] Marriage is "an affair of honour".[9]

[4] *The Superstition of Divorce, CW* 4:230.
[5] Ibid., 238–39.
[6] Ibid., 229.
[7] Ibid., 233.
[8] Ibid.
[9] Ibid.

Where does this leave what we now call "free love"? Chesterton calls free love a heresy. And divorce? He calls divorce a superstition. It is "much more of a superstition than strict sacramental marriage".[10] After all, it is the advocates of divorce who attach such great significance to "a mere ceremony", the mysterious and magical rite of getting divorced.

Chesterton asks us to step back and examine the whole concept of loyalty. Most sane men admit the necessity of being loyal to one's country. The patriot may revile his country, but he must not renounce it.[11] We pretty much agree that there are some institutions to which we are permanently attached, such as nations; just as there are others to which we are temporarily attached, such as shops. We go from shop to shop searching for what we want, but we do not go from nation to nation doing this. That is because we feel a certain loyalty to our nation. Should we not feel an even greater loyalty to the family? The family is something far more fundamental and something far more free.

Chesterton reasons that if it is permissible to expect a man to be loyal to the commonwealth that has made him, should we not expect him to be loyal to the commonwealth he has himself made?[12]

He says that the vow made most freely must be the vow kept most firmly.[13] There is nothing that compares with this vow. No other oath, no stroke of the pen creates real bodies and souls.

But does the modern divorce movement discuss any of this? Does it examine the nature of a vow, the limits and objects of loyalty, the survival of the family as a small and

[10] Ibid., 235.
[11] Ibid., 236.
[12] Ibid., 237.
[13] Ibid.

free state? No, we avoid those issues altogether, and instead we take a false view of "justice". We make divorce easier under the pretense that we are worried that current law is unfair to the poor, because they cannot obtain a divorce as readily as can the rich.

Normally, this would be an argument to which Chesterton, who is always the defender of the poor, would be inclined to listen with some sympathy. But not in this case. He would rather protect the poor from the divorce mentality of the rich, just as he would want to save them from the other fad indulged in by the rich: suicide.

> I fear I should, on the impulse of the moment, pull a poor clerk or artisan back by the coat-tails, if he were jumping over Shakespeare's Cliff, even if Dover sands were strewn with the remains of the dukes and bankers who had already taken the plunge.[14]

Chesterton asks why we are so anxious that the poor man should be free to get a divorce, and not in the least anxious that he should be free to get anything else? Why are the same people who are happy when the poor man gets a divorce horrified when he takes a drink or smokes a cigarette?[15]

> [A man] is less and less allowed to go to look for a new job; why is he allowed to go to look for a new wife?... Why must he love as he pleases; when he may not even live as he pleases?[16]

It is the same spirit that takes away the poor man's children under the pretense of order that takes away his wife under the pretense of liberty. Chesterton asks why we are so anxious

[14] Ibid., 239.
[15] Ibid., 240.
[16] Ibid., 240–41.

to break up homes that are thought to be unhappy—and not all anxious "to break up the much more unhappy factory"?[17]

> Capitalism ... is at war with the family, for the same reason which has led to its being at war with the Trade Union.... It desires its victims to be individuals, or (in other words) to be atoms. For the word atom, in its clearest meaning (which is none too clear) might be translated as "individual." If there be any bond, if there be any brotherhood, if there be any class loyalty or domestic discipline, by which the poor can help the poor, these emancipators will certainly strive to loosen that bond or lift that discipline in the most liberal fashion ... in other words smash it to atoms.
>
> The masters of modern plutocracy know what they are about.... A very profound and precise instinct has led them to single out the human household as the chief obstacle to their inhuman progress. Without the family we are helpless before the State, which in our modern case is the Servile State.[18]

The cultures and countries that historically have been the most vigorous and resilient have been those with strong families. They have had a strong domestic life. Chesterton points out that this is exactly the opposite of the myth made by modern literature, that the home is "a doll's house" and the wife a kept woman, like a doll, the mere plaything of the man. According to this myth, it is only the strong woman who breaks out of the home as if it were a prison. But in the great nations, the home is not regarded as a prison, but truly a castle, and the woman is its queen. The strong woman defends her home above all else, turning household tools into weapons if she has to and pouring boiling water from

[17] Ibid.
[18] Ibid., 241–42.

the windows on anyone or anything that dares attack the home. But modern literature portrays domesticity as tyrannical or hypocritical or boring. That does not describe domesticity. It describes the decay of domesticity. And the modern and morbid weakness is to give up, "sacrificing the normal to the abnormal".[19]

The family should be the strongest institution in a society—and traditionally it has been—because it is the one institution that people build spontaneously for themselves. As Chesterton says, it is "a small and free state".[20] It is the only state that creates and loves its own citizens, yet like so many other small kingdoms, it is under attack. It is besieged. Its enemies seek to destroy the family. They work to have the State take over the functions of the family by a day-care system that makes the mother irrelevant or a welfare system that makes the father irrelevant. They also try to destroy the family simply by redefining it. The people who do this, says Chesterton, are detached, disgruntled, and drifting. They are always making an

> excuse for altering what is common, corporate, traditional and popular. And the alteration is always for the worse.[21]

This revolt against the family is utterly unnatural, a revolt against nature itself and the natural attraction between father and mother. This natural attraction is called a child. It is a simple truth that the modern world insists on ignoring.

> There is no dispute about the purpose of Nature in creating such an attraction. It would be more intelligent to call it the purpose of God; for Nature can have no purpose unless God is behind it. To talk of the purpose of Nature is to make a

[19] Ibid., 247.
[20] Ibid., 238.
[21] Ibid., 249.

vain attempt to avoid being anthropomorphic, merely by being feminist. It is believing in a goddess because you are too
sceptical to believe in a god.[22]

A family is of course the best way to create, to protect, and
to raise children. Besides this obvious truth, Chesterton also
argues that the family must be kept intact because the home
is the greatest refuge of freedom in the world.

Divorce is not an act of freedom. On the contrary, it is an
act of slavery. A society where vows can be easily broken is
not a free society. A free society cannot function without
volunteers keeping their commitments to each other. And a
free society cannot function without its most basic unit, the
family, being kept intact, but it can only be kept together
freely, by an act of the will, by volunteers keeping their vows.

Chesterton anticipates the objections from the proponents of divorce to his characterization of divorce as an act
of slavery. But he reminds them that anyone who has ever
read *Uncle Tom's Cabin* knows that one of the oldest and simplest charges against slavery was that it broke up families.[23]

We need laws that support the family and keep it together,
but we also need an economic system that does not put such
pressure on families that they crack apart. When people are isolated and divided, they are weak. Then they are easy to ex-
ploit by both big government and big business.

Chesterton says that the two greatest enemies to freedom
and to the family in our society are big government and big
business. Families are a nuisance to businesses that have to
provide a living wage, health care plans, and maternity leave,
and that have to put up with employees coming in late or
going home early because a child is sick or missed the school

[22] Ibid., 253.
[23] Ibid., 270.

bus. And families are a nuisance to the State because they interfere with regulation and standardization and officialism. Traditionally, the State has been subordinate to the family, but when the family loses its strength, the government gains extraordinary power over people's personal lives.

Nowhere is this more evident than in education. Education used to be the domain of the parent; now it is the domain of the State. The State has great power, but its authority is something anonymous and vague and invisible. It works through the State education system, from kindergarten to the huge State universities. It is a faceless network that tells people what to think. It sponsors scientific research that supports theories that not only defy common sense, but also defy the authority of the parent. Chesterton calls this "officialism". Officialism is the direct enemy of traditional authority.

> For the modern world will accept no dogmas upon any authority; but it will accept any dogmas on no authority. Say that a thing is so, according to the Pope or the Bible, and it will be dismissed as a superstition without examination. But preface your remark merely with "they say" or "don't you know that?" or try (and fail) to remember the name of some professor mentioned in some newspaper; and the keen rationalism of the modern mind will accept every word you say.[24]

One of the things "they say" is that when most marriages end, they end "by mutual consent". Chesterton disagrees. He says that in most divorces, only one person wants the divorce.[25] There may be unhappy marriages, but there are no happy divorces.

[24] Ibid., 257–58.
[25] Ibid., 276.

The divorce controversy is less about divorce than about remarriage. This is where the superstition comes in. People think divorce is a ceremony that will undo a vow they have made so that they can make the vow again. As Chesterton says, they want to have their wedding cake and eat it, too.[26] And we have now created a system where this is possible. We now reward a man for deserting his wife by letting him have another wife. We never encourage him to go back to the woman he first chose from all the women in the world.

Chesterton says we have to get away from the poisonous modern philosophies and back to the primary things, the permanent things. We have to honor the family above the State and, more importantly, above the office or the factory. And we begin to honor the family by honoring marriage.

> We know there is a school of prigs who disapprove of the wine [at the wedding at Cana in Galilee]; and there may now be a school of prigs who disapprove of the wedding. For in ... the story of Cana, ... the pedants are prejudiced against the earthly elements as much as, or more than, the heavenly elements. It is not the supernatural that disgusts them, so much as the natural. And those of us who have seen all the normal rules and relations of humanity uprooted by random speculators, as if they were abnormal abuses and almost accidents, will understand why men have sought for something divine if they wished to preserve anything human. They will know why common sense, cast out from some academy of fads and fashions ..., has age after age sought refuge in the high sanity of a sacrament.[27]

Chesterton has made several arguments against divorce, but he has deliberately left out the loftiest argument—that mar-

[26] Ibid., 272.
[27] Ibid., 288.

riage is a divine institution—because he says anyone who believes that would not believe in divorce. He is not asking anyone assume the worth of his creed, but simply to consider the worth of the claims made by modern society. He asks those who are so caught up in defending divorce: What do they really finally expect for themselves and for their children?[28]

Father, mother, and child, says Chesterton, form a sacred triangle that cannot be destroyed. It will only destroy the civilization that disregards it. And the Church has held up a mystical mirror to that sacred triangle in which the order of the three things is reversed, a holy family of child, mother, and father.[29]

[28] Ibid., 290.
[29] Ibid., 261.

13

Eugenics and Other Evils

The modern world is insane, not so much because it admits the abnormal as because it cannot recover the normal.

—*Eugenics and Other Evils*

G. K. Chesterton said that we cannot recover the normal because we have created a culture that is at "war with the older culture of Christendom".[1] We are caught up in a "modern craze for scientific officialism and strict social organization".[2] And the problem with the official scientists is that they become steadily less scientific and more official.

The book *Eugenics and Other Evils* was published in 1922, but Chesterton had written most of it ten years earlier. He was hoping there would be no need to publish such a book and that he could just throw his notes into the fire. Instead, he found that the issue had not gone away, nor had any of his arguments gone out of date. Unfortunately, this book still has not gone out of date. Chesterton's arguments remain as valid as ever. We are still faced with what he called "the same

[1] *Eugenics and Other Evils, CW* 4:293.
[2] Ibid.

stuffy science, the same bullying bureaucracy and the same terrorism by tenth-rate professors".[3] Think about those words: bullying, terrorism, tenth-rate professors. Our friend G. K. Chesterton could be a very funny man, but he was also not afraid to show his anger, and show it as articulately as his mirth. While this book is perhaps a prime example of his anger, we can also argue that he was slow to anger, since he withheld it for ten years before unleashing it.

The book is not dated in spite of the fact that the term "eugenics" *is* dated. So before we examine Chesterton's book, some background information is in order.

The term "eugenics" was coined in the nineteenth century by an Englishman named Francis Galton. He advocated "the betterment of mankind".[4] Sounds good. He wanted to improve the physical and mental makeup of human beings. Sounds good. How did he intend to accomplish this? By increasing the proportion of those people with "superior genetic endowment". Sounds suspicious. How did he envision increasing the proportion of people with "superior genetic endowment"? By selective breeding. Sounds a little terrifying. Also sounds a little familiar. Where did he get his ideas? This will sound *very* familiar. He got his ideas from his cousin: Charles Darwin. Galton not only gave credit to Darwin for his own ideas about eugenics, but Darwin repaid the favor by referring to Galton's ideas about human breeding in his book *The Descent of Man*. Darwin called Galton's work "admirable"[5] and agreed with him that the "inferior" members

[3] Ibid., 294.

[4] Francis Galton, *Hereditary Genius: An Inquiry into Its Laws and Consequences* (1869), preface.

[5] Charles Darwin, *The Descent of Man* in *Darwin: A Norton Critical Edition*, ed. Philip Appleman (New York: W. W. Norton, 1970), 223.

of society should not marry because they might supplant the "better" members of society.[6]

There were many advocates of eugenics here in America, but probably the most prominent was the woman who founded the organization that became Planned Parenthood: Margaret Sanger. Margaret Sanger is hailed by some today as a pioneer defender of women's rights. Perhaps more than any other person in the twentieth century, she is responsible for the widespread distribution of contraceptives and the mundane acceptance of "birth control".

What is less known about her is that her motives for advocating birth control had less to do with "sexual freedom" than with eugenics. Anyone who doubts this simply has to read the journal she founded and edited for many years, *The Birth Control Review*. In 1919, she proclaimed in the *Review*, "More children for the fit, less for the unfit." By "fit", she meant the privileged, the brainy, and the white—people like herself. She said she wanted to use birth control to create "a race of thoroughbreds". By "unfit", she meant not only the physically handicapped and the mentally retarded, but also, specifically, "Hebrews, Slavs, Catholics, and Negroes". She targeted these groups as threats because of their increasing numbers. She worked hard to set up most of her birth-control clinics in urban neighborhoods populated by these groups. She openly suggested that parents should apply to have babies "as immigrants have to apply for visas".[7]

Margaret Sanger was also a member of the American Eugenics Society, which successfully lobbied for sterilization laws that targeted society's undesirables and unwanted. These

---

[6] Ibid., 275.

[7] Quoted in Mary Senander, "Eugenics Part of Sanger Legacy", *Star Tribune*, October 14, 1993, 19A.

laws were passed in more than half the states in the U.S. and led to several cases of forced sterilization.[8]

Why do not we hear of this connection between Margaret Sanger, the founder of Planned Parenthood, and eugenics?

In case you have not already figured it out, there was another famous person who advocated eugenics: Adolf Hitler. He did more than just lobby for eugenics, he officially instituted it. He led an entire country in carrying out its principles, not only to breed what he believed to be a superior race, but to eliminate everyone whom he considered to be inferior. And where did Hitler find plenty of support for his eugenic ideas? From Margaret Sanger and her circle. Eugenic scientists from Nazi Germany wrote articles for Sanger's *Birth Control Review*, and members of Sanger's American Birth Control League visited Nazi Germany, sat in on sessions of the Supreme Eugenics Court, and returned with glowing reports of how the sterilization law was "weeding out the worst strains in the Germanic stock in a scientific and truly humanitarian way".[9]

Needless to say, after World War II, when all the terrible truth about Nazi Germany came out, when the world learned of the horrors of the Holocaust and the death camps, the term eugenics was utterly discredited. Margaret Sanger was quick to distance herself from eugenics and began to emphasize birth control as merely a feminist issue. And now we do not hear about eugenics at all.

Unfortunately, the philosophy behind eugenics is with us still. Generally speaking, all of the original arguments in favor of eugenics have become the same arguments in favor of birth control, abortion, and euthanasia.

[8] Ibid.
[9] Robert Marshall and Charles Donovan, *Blessed Are the Barren: The Social Policy of Planned Parenthood* (San Francisco: Ignatius Press, 1991), 277–78.

Chesterton understood this. But he understood it in 1912. As with so many other things, Chesterton saw exactly what we see. Only he saw it long before it happened. The very title "Eugenics and Other Evils" obviously implies that eugenics is an evil, and one connected to other evils. When Chesterton attacks something that is evil, his attack is always wrapped around a defense of what is good. He is concerned that we have lost sight of what is good. We have even lost sight of what is normal. We have lost our common sense.

What is normal is this: a man and a woman fall in love, get married, and have a family. For thousands of years, men and women have been able to figure this normal thing out for themselves. This basic human freedom was part of the common experience.

The early proponents of eugenics defied this common sense by saying that men and women should not marry for love but, rather, for good breeding. They said people should not risk having children who might be handicapped or ill or weak. In other words, says Chesterton, they should not risk having children who turn out to be John Keats or Robert Louis Stevenson. In a chilling prophecy of the abortion mentality, Chesterton says that the eugenicists have an attitude toward the unborn child that was in every other age unthinkable: "They seek his life to take it away." [10] They also have precisely the wrong idea of the purpose of medicine:

> We call in the doctor to save us from death; and, death being admittedly an evil, he has the right to administer the ... most recondite pill which he may think is a cure for all such menaces of death. He has not the right to administer death as the cure for all human ills. [11]

[10] *Eugenics and Other Evils*, *CW* 4:369.
[11] Ibid., 322.

The normal person has always known that preventing the birth of a baby is a highly unnatural act, no matter how it is done. But it is made to sound harmless and even sensible when it is called "eugenic" or when it is called birth control or when it is called reproductive freedom. But anyone who cannot see the real evil behind such terms is what Chesterton calls a "splendid dupe".

> Evil always takes advantage of ambiguity.... Evil always wins through the strength of its splendid dupes; and there has in all ages been a disastrous alliance between abnormal innocence and abnormal sin.[12]

The only way to explain what happened in Nazi Germany is that evil won through the strength of its splendid dupes: too many people thought they were doing a good thing because they believed a lie. A lie that sounded good because it was called patriotic and was supported by the scientific officialism of the regime. It is also the only way to explain what has happened in this country for the last three decades. Millions of people have believed an incredibly evil lie. A lie that sounds good because it is called "choice". A lie that sounds even better when it has scientific officialism behind it.

Two University of Chicago economists recently published a study[13] that showed that the reduction in crime rates in the 1990s can be linked to the legalization of abortion in the 1970s. You see, the women who would have given birth to criminals instead had abortions, so we had fewer criminals on the street. There you go. A new kind of crime prevention. Preventing criminals from being born. Never mind

---

[12] Ibid., 297.
[13] John J. Donohue and Steven D. Levitt, "Legalized Abortion and Crime", Working Papers of the Northwestern University/University of Chicago Joint Center for Poverty Research, October 1, 1999.

the grotesque implications of these conclusions, including overt racism. The experts have shown a statistical link between lower crime rates and higher abortion rates.

Statistics. In a 1905 column in the *Illustrated London News* Chesterton gave us some guidance about statistics.

> It is an error to suppose that statistics are merely untrue. They are also wicked. As used today, they serve the purpose of making masses of men feel helpless and cowardly.... And I have another quarrel with statistics. I believe that even when they are correct they are entirely misleading.... It is psychologically impossible, in short, when we hear real scientific statistics, not to think that they mean something. Generally they mean nothing. Sometimes they mean something that isn't true.[14]

Let us go back, way back to Darwin's cousin, Francis Galton, the man who gave us the term "eugenics". Before Galton wrote about breeding geniuses, he was famous for something else. He was considered a pioneer in the study of statistics.[15]

He would be pleased with his legacy. Lying by numbers is as elementary as painting by numbers. When organizations such as Planned Parenthood and the United Nations Population Fund spread their gospel of contraception throughout the world, the main scare tactic they use is numbers. They use statistics about poverty. They use statistics to show that poor people will have lots of babies who will also be poor, which will increase poverty. So, naturally the only way to prevent more poverty is to prevent poor people from having children.

---

[14] *ILN*, November 18, 1905, *CW* 27:61–62.

[15] Galton published several books and papers on applied statistics, including *Statistical Inquiries into the Efficacy of Prayer* (1872), which of course proved statistically that prayer is not effective at all. So there you go.

Chesterton predicted exactly what would happen if the eugenics mentality was allowed to take hold. It would mean an attack on the poorest and most helpless in society, "a war upon the weak".[16] Obviously abortion attacks the most defenseless of all people: babies. But the international politics of birth control preys on the poor and underprivileged throughout the world, forcing them to accept birth control in exchange for their basic needs.

Chesterton was right in his prediction. And since he was right, it might do us well to look at where he placed the blame for this tragic set of events. This is where we get into the "other evils". Sometimes it is too easy to demonize abortionists and feminists and advocates of birth control. Even though they must be actively opposed, and Chesterton did oppose them, he would argue that they are not the main players. There is a much bigger problem that must be dealt with. There is a much greater evil that must be eliminated.

The fact that babies are unwanted goes back to the fact that our society has created a whole class of people that are unwanted. They are the permanently poor. They represent all races and creeds and colors. They are:

> people of every physical and mental type, of every sort of health and breeding. . . . They have nothing in common but the wrong we do them.[17]

Chesterton says these people have been utterly exploited, used like tools and used up like tools. They have no hope of getting property, of getting enough capital to support themselves or a family. Chesterton also understands clearly that:

---

[16] *Eugenics and Other Evils, CW* 4:337.
[17] Ibid., 390.

The situation was aggravated by the fact that these sexual pleasures were often the only ones the very poor could obtain, and were, therefore, disproportionately pursued.[18]

Then, the privileged class, which has so benefited from capitalism at the expense of the underprivileged class, has a drastic solution: Poor people should not have babies.

We do not like to think about this. Our society does not like to face the problems of injustice because it usually interferes with business. Chesterton says:

Prosperity does not favour self-examination.[19]

The average business man began to be agnostic, not so much because he did not know where he was, as because he wanted to forget. Many of the rich took to scepticism exactly as the poor took to drink; because it was a way out.[20]

He laments the breaking of the tools of Mammon much more than the breaking of the images of God.... No one seems able to imagine capitalist industrialism being sacrificed to any other object.... People miss the main thing and concentrate on the mean thing. "Modern conditions" are treated as fixed, though the very word "modern" implies that they are fugitive. "Old ideas" are treated as impossible, though their very antiquity often proves their permanence....

I could fill this book with examples of the universal, unconscious assumption that life and sex must live by the laws of "business" or industrialism, and not *vice versa*.[21]

Wealth, and the social science supported by wealth, had tried an inhuman experiment. The experiment had entirely failed. They sought to make wealth accumulate—and they made

[18] Ibid., 381.
[19] Ibid., 385.
[20] Ibid., 377.
[21] Ibid., 385–86.

men decay. Then instead of confessing the error, and trying to restore the wealth, or attempting to repair the decay, they are trying to cover their first cruel experiment with a more cruel experiment.[22]

We must hasten to point out that the evil of big business has an evil twin sister: big government. When government tries to right the wrongs created by capitalism, it creates an even worse mess. The idea of socialism may sound good: to provide houses and food for everyone. However, in order to carry this out, State officials would have to inspect houses and regulate meals. The State has found it easier, Chesterton points out, to provide the building inspectors without providing the builders, and easier to restrict the diet without providing the dinner. We have simply "added all the bureaucratic tyrannies of a Socialist state to the old plutocratic tyrannies of a Capitalist State".[23] The result is a loss of liberty and an assault on the common man.

The government official will gain enormous power in a system that is obsessed with regulation, using the excuse that "the health of the community" is being protected. Chesterton says that using this excuse, the official will soon "control all the habits of all the citizens, and among the rest their habits in the matter of sex". Then the most private matters will come under public scrutiny.

> If a man's personal health is a public concern, his most private acts are *more* public than his most public acts.[24]

When the State starts meddling with our primary habits, or, as Chesterton says, when all law begins, so to speak, "next

[22] Ibid., 392.
[23] Ibid., 404.
[24] Ibid., 397.

to the skin or nearest to the vitals", then it is obvious that the laws will soon assault marriage and motherhood.[25]

We find ourselves in this condition because we have lost our perspective. Chesterton says we have forgotten "the first things".

> The first things must be the very fountains of life, love and birth and babyhood; and these are always covered fountains, flowing in the quiet courts of the home.[26]

The home and the family must be protected and must not be interfered with by the State. It was an industrialist and materialist society, says Chesterton, that has been responsible for producing so many unhappy marriages because it produced so many unhappy men. But all the government reforms have been aimed at rescuing the industrialism and the materialism rather than the happiness. We have sacrificed "the ancient uses of things because they do not fit in with the modern abuses".[27]

The point about eugenics and the other evils that sprang from it is that they propose to eliminate poverty simply by eliminating people. Chesterton's solution is not as simple, but it is the right one. The way to eliminate poor people is to eliminate their poverty, so that they are not poor anymore, but are still people. They deserve enough property and capital and liberty so that they can keep their families and their dignity. They are the image of God, and they must not be broken.

[25] Ibid., 399.
[26] Ibid., 398.
[27] Ibid., 407.

14

Father Brown

The true object of an intelligent detective story is not to baffle the reader, but to enlighten the reader; but to enlighten him in such a manner that each successive portion of the truth comes as a surprise. In this, as in much nobler types of mystery, the object of the true mystic is not merely to mystify, but to illuminate.

—*Illustrated London News*, August 28, 1920

G. K. Chesterton once wrote:

I should enjoy nothing more than always writing detective stories, except always reading them.[1]

The man who so loved detective fiction gave us one of its most delightful characters. A character who was in many ways like Chesterton himself, which is not exactly surprising. He was paradoxical, humble, intuitive, charitable, lovable, and always in touch with the truth.

He was also quite different from Chesterton. He was short and silent and almost unnoticeable, and he was a priest. His name was Father Brown.

[1] *The Thing, CW* 3:136.

When Chesterton said he loved to read detective stories, he was not exaggerating. He read them by the hundreds. He usually had his pockets stuffed with them. He would pick one from the bookstall at the railway station and start reading it while he waited for the next train. Usually he would miss the train. Then he would wander off reading the book and forget to pay for it. Fortunately, the bookseller was quite used to this scenario and would simply send Mrs. Chesterton the bill.

Chesterton said that the detective story differs from every other story in this: that the reader is only happy if he feels like a fool.[2] In the mystery tale we are suddenly confronted with a truth that we have never suspected but all at once realize to be true. The sharp transition from ignorance, he says, is good for humility. And the sharp transition from ignorance is also something quite similar to the religious experience known as revelation.

Besides being a reader of detective stories, Chesterton was also a writer of detective stories. He created a number of interesting and amusing detectives, from the poet Gabriel Gale to the bureaucrat Mr. Pond. But there was one detective who surpassed all of Chesterton's other literary creations: the "little Norfolk priest", Father Brown. Now, if you enjoy detective stories, it is likely that you already know who Father Brown is. If you have never heard of Father Brown, then I have the pleasure of introducing him to you. But first, a little explanation is in order.

Even if you do not read detective stories, you have of course heard of Sherlock Holmes. It was that brilliant but eccentric "consulting detective" who, with his sidekick, Dr. Watson,

[2] *ILN*, October 25, 1930.

dominated the landscape of detective fiction at the beginning of the twentieth century. Every fiction magazine had to have its own version of Sherlock Holmes.

And that was a problem. How could any writer hope to equal, much less surpass, Sherlock Holmes? The very excellence and popularity of the Holmes stories had led detective fiction into a dead-end street. Writers competed with one another to invent a crime-solver more logical than Holmes, or a detective more observant than Holmes, or an amateur sleuth more eccentric than Holmes. They battled one another at contriving ever more baffling crimes and still more convoluted puzzles.

It was Chesterton who came to the rescue with a whole new character and a whole new approach. Chesterton admired the Sherlock Holmes stories greatly. But he was not happy with the fact that the rest of detective fiction consisted only of poor imitations of Sherlock Holmes. Chesterton was the first critic of detective fiction to insist on fair play for the reader. He objected to the unlikely endings that trick the poor reader by revealing something at the end of the story about which the author had not given the slightest hint along the way. He loved being surprised to learn that the countess had killed the professor. But he hated to be introduced to the countess for the first time at the very tail end of the story.

He also disliked the artificial emphasis on the details and minutia of the crime and the investigation. Such a formulaic approach was boring, sterile, and dispiriting. He wanted more of the human elements of crime—motives, emotions, choices, innocence, and guilt.

> I think ... the worst thing even in the best shockers is ... connected with ... a certain mechanical or materialistic

interpretation of human interest. . . . The curate, let us say, confesses that he jumped over an incredibly high wall to murder the grandmother; and the professor of psychology [says he dreamed it]. . . . Then, when we think that the curate is cleared and out of it, we are relieved to find in the last chapter that he is the criminal after all; both he and the author having concealed up to this moment the fact that the curate held the International Championship for the High Jump.

This method . . . pursues the highly legitimate aim of shifting the spot-light from the guilty to the innocent. And yet I think that it fails, and that there is a reason for its failure. The error is the materialistic error: the mistake of supposing that our interest in the plot is mechanical, when it is really moral. But art is never unmoral, though it is sometimes immoral; that is, moral with the wrong morality. The only thrill, even of a common thriller, is concerned somehow with the conscience and the will. It involves finding out that men are worse or better than they seem, and that by their own choice. Therefore, there can never be quite so much excitement over the mere mechanical truth of how a man managed to do something difficult, as over the mere fact that he wanted to do it.[3]

Chesterton insisted that readers ultimately want enlightenment, not mystification, and that the heart of every complicated detective yarn must be the discovery of a simple truth—a discovery someone might yell from an upstairs window, like "The Archdeacon is Bloody Bill!"[4]

Chesterton knew *he* enjoyed being fooled, and he argued that all detective story readers want to be fooled, but fooled fairly. He favored the cozy mystery, the domestic murder, with a millionaire usually performing the important service of being the murder victim and the scope of the investiga-

---

[3] Ibid., July 28, 1934.
[4] Ibid., August 19, 1922, *CW* 32:431.

tion narrowed to limited time, limited space, and a limited number of suspects, with all the clues revealed to the reader as well as to the detective.

Now, it is a fine thing to have a theory of the detective story, and Chesterton's theories were indeed influential. But he did more than theorize. He showed the way.

Chesterton made Father Brown's appearance as commonplace and conventional as possible. The priest was a short little man with a moon face and blinking, owlish eyes. He wore a black cassock, a clerical shovel hat, and he carried a large, shabby black umbrella. He was a companionable man who could be engaging and witty in conversation, and—very importantly—he was an attentive and sympathetic listener. The Father Brown stories avoid the clichés and stereotypes of all those imitation Sherlock Holmes cases. Father Brown never visits a den of thieves or raids the headquarters of a professional criminal gang. He finds his adventures in the comfort of a restaurant, or in a middle-class home, or in the courtyard of a Gothic church. And while every detective must use evidence to solve the mystery, Father Brown's talent is not his ability to identify the telltale cigar ash or to interpret the peculiar footprints. It is his ability to understand the human heart.

> I can always grasp moral evidence more easily than the other sorts. I go by a man's eyes and voice ... and whether his family seems happy, and by what subject he chooses—and avoids.[5]

> If you want to know what a lady is really like, don't look at her; for she may be too clever for you. Don't look at the

men round her, for they may be too silly about her. But look
at some other woman who is always near to her, and especially one who is under her. You will see in that mirror her
real face.[6]

Father Brown's moral reasoning plays a part in every one of
his stories. It is the key to solving the crime. Of course, it
is also the reflection of Chesterton's own moral reasoning,
and that is why these stories have such a surprising depth of
meaning.

But how exactly does "moral reasoning" solve crimes?

Now, I can tell you about Father Brown and about his
methods, but there is one thing I cannot do. I cannot give
away the ending of any of the stories. Chesterton said that
the man who tells the ending of a detective story "is simply
a wicked man, as wicked as the man who deliberately breaks
a child's soap-bubble—and he is more wicked than Nero".[7]
He destroys "one human pleasure so that it can never be
recovered". Obviously such a person belongs down in the
lowest circle of hell, where Dante put other traitors.

In order to explain how moral reasoning can solve a crime,
I am going to tell you the ending of one of the stories.

I just will not tell you which one.

And I will not tell you who the murderer is.

I will just tell you how Father Brown solved the crime.
Better yet, I will let Father Brown himself tell you:

You see, it was I who killed all those people.

I ... murdered them all myself. So, of course, I knew how
it was done. I ... planned out each of the crimes very carefully. I ... thought out exactly how a thing like that could be
done, and in what style or state of mind a man could really

---

[6] "The Actor and the Alibi", ibid., 524.
[7] *ILN*, November 7, 1908, *CW* 28:210.

do it. And when I was quite sure that I felt exactly like the murderer myself, of course I knew who he was. . . .

No, no, I don't mean just a figure of speech. . . . I mean that I really did see myself . . . committing the murders. I didn't actually kill the men . . . ; but that's not the point. . . . I mean that I thought and thought about how a man might come to be like that, until I realized that I really *was* like that in everything except actual final consent to the action. It was once suggested to me by a friend of mine, as a sort of religious exercise. I believe he got it from Pope Leo XIII, who was always rather a hero of mine. . . .

I [try] to clear my mind of such elements of sanity and constructive common sense as I have had the luck to learn or inherit. I shut down and [darken] all the skylights through which comes the good daylight out of heaven. . . . That is just where this little religious exercise is so wholesome. . . . No man's really any good till he knows how bad he is, or might be; till he's realized exactly how much right he has to all this snobbery, and sneering, and talking about 'criminals' as if they were apes in a forest.[8]

The first twelve Father Brown stories began appearing in the United States in *The Saturday Evening Post* in 1910. When these were collected and published in book form as *The Innocence of Father Brown*, they created a sensation. Ellery Queen called it "the Miracle Book of 1911".

Everyone immediately recognized that the Father Brown stories were breaking new ground. Chesterton's approach brought motive and character back into prominence in detective fiction and freed these stories from the imitative techniques of the rivals of Sherlock Holmes. He certainly captured the attention of the leading mystery writers of his day. They embraced his new style of murder mystery. They began

---

[8] What are you looking here for? I told you I would not tell you which story this passage came from.

writing stories of domestic crimes with human motives, with a limited list of suspects, with obvious (though well-disguised) clues, and with an unlikely detective who solves his puzzles without relying on superhuman knowledge or intelligence. Indeed, whenever you think of the great detectives of mystery fiction's golden age—Hercule Poirot, Lord Peter Wimsey, Miss Marple, Ellery Queen, Philo Vance, or Nero Wolfe—remember their parentage. Remember that they had a father. His name was Father Brown.

And there is another famous detective who was clearly inspired by Father Brown. Like Father Brown, he was slightly comical and improbable, unassuming, unthreatening, never taken seriously by the guilty party, but always knowing much more than he let on. I am speaking, of course, of TV's *Columbo*.

But who was the inspiration for Father Brown? Chesterton wrote over fifty Father Brown stories. But you may be surprised to learn that he wrote almost half of them *before* he became a Catholic. It was a real Roman Catholic priest, however, who served as the model for Father Brown. It was this same priest, Father John O'Connor, who also played an instrumental role in Chesterton's conversion.

I cannot do better than tell the story of how the first notion of this detective comedy came into my mind.

In those early days, ... it was my fate to wander over many parts of England, delivering what were politely called lectures.... In the course of such wanderings ... [I] stayed the night with a leading citizen ... who had assembled a group of local friends ... including the curate of the Roman Catholic Church; a small man with a smooth face and a demure but elfish expression. I was struck by the tact and humour with which he mingled with his very Yorkshire and very Protestant company; and I soon found out they had, in their bluff way, already learned to appreciate him as something of a character.... I liked him very much; but if you had told me that ten years afterwards I should be a Mormon Missionary in the Cannibal Islands, I should not have been more surprised than at the suggestion that, fully fifteen years afterwards, I should be making to him my General Confession and being received into the Church that he served.

Next morning he and I walked over ... the moors.... I mentioned to the priest in conversation that I proposed to support in print a certain proposal ... in connection with some rather sordid social questions of vice and crime. On this particular point he thought I was in error, or rather in ignorance, as indeed I was. And, merely as a necessary duty and to prevent me from falling into a mare's nest, he told me certain facts he knew about perverted practices.... I had not imagined that the world could hold such horrors.... When we returned to the house we found it was full of visitors, and fell into special conversation with two hearty and healthy young Cambridge undergraduates.... They began to discuss music and landscape with my friend Father O'Connor.... The talk soon deepened into a discussion on matters more philosophical and moral; and when the priest had left the room, the two young men broke out into generous expressions of admiration.... Then there fell a curious reflective silence, at the end of which one of the undergraduates suddenly burst out, "All the same, I don't believe his sort of life is the right one. It's all very well to like religious music and so on, when you're all shut up in a sort of cloister and don't know anything about the real evil in the world. But ... I believe in a fellow coming out into the world, and facing the evil that's in it, and knowing something about the dangers and all that. It's a very beautiful thing to be innocent and ignorant, but I think it's a much finer thing not to be afraid of knowledge."

To me, still almost shivering with the appalling ... facts of which the priest had warned me, this comment came with such a colossal and crushing irony, that I nearly burst into a loud harsh laugh in the drawing-room. For I knew perfectly well that, as regards all the solid Satanism which the priest knew and warred against with all his life, these two Cambridge gentlemen (luckily for them) knew about as much of real evil as two babies.[9]

When Chesterton understood that the priest was far more knowledgeable of the "real world" than the smug intellectuals ever imagined, he had the makings of his fictional priest-detective. It was typical of Chesterton's style to turn set expectations on their heads.

It is precisely such expectations that have helped the readers of these stories feel so marvelously fooled. When the truth comes as a surprise, that is what makes it marvelous. And there is something else surprising about these stories. People have been drawn to them, not because Father Brown is a priest, but because he is a detective. However, what is really most interesting about Father Brown is not that he is a detective, but that he is a priest. Because he is a priest, Father Brown understands that every man can be a murderer, but also that every man can be a saint. He can expose a false priest because the imposter attacks reason, and the real priest knows that the Church defends reason.

> Reason is from God, and when things are unreasonable there is something the matter.[10]

He understands that reason is tied to justice. But also that justice is tied to mercy. Father Brown is certainly concerned with solving the crime, but more importantly with saving

---

[9] *Autobiography*, *CW* 16:314–18.

[10] "The Red Moon of Meru", *Penguin Complete Father Brown*, 565. But I did not give anything away because this is not the story where the false priest attacks reason.

the soul of the criminal. Chesterton clearly understands the
gravity of what it is that a priest must do. The rest of the
world does not. The rest of the world, as Father Brown says,
"will only pardon sins that they don't really think are sinful".[11]

People often ask me what is the best introduction to Chesterton. I have many answers to the question. In fact, my
answers to that question could fill a book. But certainly one
of the answers is the Father Brown stories. They are full of
Chesterton's wit and wisdom, and they are good yarns. Besides that, they are *detective* stories. Detective stories are about
finding the truth. And Chesterton understands that our search
for truth is what defines us.

> All science [he says], even the divine science, is a sublime
> detective story. Only it is not set to detect why a man is
> dead; but the darker secret of why he is alive.[12]

[11] "The Chief Mourner of Marne", ibid., 583.
[12] *The Thing, CW* 3:191.

15

Conclusion: Chesterton for Today

> A society is in decay when common sense has become uncommon.
>
> —*G.K.'s Weekly*, November 2, 1933

G. K. Chesterton said that humanity has passed through every sort of storm and shipwreck, but for the first time we are confused about which is the storm and which is the shipwreck, and which is the ship and what we are rescuing from what.[1] We are confused because we have lost our common sense.

Since this is the concluding chapter, let us talk about making conclusions. What sets Chesterton apart from most modern thinkers is that he makes conclusions. He speaks with confidence, but not with arrogance, about what he believes. He is willing to take a stand and say what the truth is. He is also willing to say what the modern mistakes and errors are. And one of the greatest errors of the modern world is that it will not admit its errors. There is a vague idea that *every* idea is good. As Chesterton says, the modern mind cannot make

---

[1] *New York Herald Tribune Magazine*, July 5, 1931.

up its mind. The modern mind thinks the greatest of virtues is to be "open-minded". But Chesterton says that the human mind is designed to come to conclusions, and if it does not do that, it is not doing its job.[2]

An open mind is really a mark of foolishness, like an open mouth.[3]

The object of opening the mind, as of opening the mouth, is to shut it again on something solid.[4]

In this book we have called Chesterton the Apostle of Common Sense. We could also have called him an evangelist, for he is certainly a bringer of good news, of uproariously good news. He shows us that laughter is divine; it is the shout of joy among the sons of men. But we also could have called Chesterton a prophet. Chesterton's words ring with a wisdom and insight that is not his own. Anyone who sits late at his banquets knows without doubt that something infinitely greater than he speaks through him, in the very same sense as that which we recite in the Creed, that God, "has spoken through the prophets".

Chesterton was also a prophet in that he described human events before they unfolded. Again and again he revealed a foresight that can only be described as prophetic. If we were to compile these "prophecies", it would be an amazing list.

Chesterton died three years before the beginning of World War II, but he warned against Hitler before anyone else.[5] He warned that there would be an outbreak of violence against

---

[2] *Heretics*, *CW* 1:196.
[3] *ILN*, October 10, 1908, *CW* 28:196.
[4] *Autobiography*, *CW* 16:212.
[5] For instance, *ILN*, December 19, 1931.

the Jews.[6] He accurately predicted that the war would come, that it would begin on the Polish border,[7] and that it would be the most horrible war in history.[8] Long before that, he saw that the airplane would totally change warfare, leading to war conducted not just against soldiers but innocent civilians.[9] He recognized that technology, which is always advertised as being for our betterment, can just as easily be used to improve ways of killing people.[10]

He said that as an industrial society we would use electricity, water power, oil, and so on, to reduce the work imposed on each of us to a minimum. But the machine would become our master. And technology would create as many problems as it solved.[11]

> The same modern industrial civilisation, which aims at rapidity, also produces congestion.[12]

> The modern world is a crowd of very rapid-racing cars all brought to a standstill and stuck in a block of traffic.[13]

> Civilization has run on ahead of the soul of man and is producing faster than he can think and give thanks.[14]

> We have thought of many ways of going to the North Pole, and we may yet think of some way of going to the other side

---

[6] For instance, ibid., February 28, 1914 (*CW* 30:50–53); September 4, 1920 (*CW* 32:81–85); and *The New Jerusalem*, *CW* 20:191–92.

[7] *ILN*, September 24, 1932.

[8] Ibid., December 2, 1933.

[9] *The Outline of Sanity*, *CW* 5:64.

[10] Ibid., 158.

[11] *ILN*, March 21, 1925, *CW* 33:522.

[12] Ibid., December 23, 1922, *CW* 32:510.

[13] Ibid., May 29, 1926, *CW* 34:98.

[14] *Daily News* February 21, 1902.

of the Moon; and there can be nothing really arresting along that line of thought except the truly arresting question of whether we particularly want to go there. An Englishman can communicate with Manhattan by wireless, and he may yet communicate with Mars by more wireless; and, in both cases, nothing remains but the deeper and darker problem of thinking of something to say.[15]

Chesterton predicted both the rise[16] *and the fall*[17] of communism in Russia. He predicted, that in the meantime, the government there would be a rigid bureaucracy,[18] that small nations would be swallowed by that empire, but would break loose again and survive the empire.[19]

And while the fears of the Western world would all focus on the godless communists in Russia, Chesterton warned that the next great heresy would be right here, and it would be an attack on morality, especially sexual morality. He said:

The madness of tomorrow is not in Moscow but much more in Manhattan.[20]

He correctly predicted that there would be "a fashionable fatalism founded on Freud".[21] He said we would at once "exalt lust and forbid fertility".[22] We would eventually be no different from the commercial centers of antiquity, like

[15] *ILN*, December 27, 1930, *CW* 35:437–38.
[16] Introduction to Gorky's *Creatures That Once Were Men*. (1905).
[17] *ILN*, July 12, 1919, *CW* 31:504.
[18] Ibid., February 1, 1919, *CW* 31:421.
[19] Ibid., July 14, 1906, *CW* 27:234.
[20] *G.K.'s Weekly*, June 19, 1926.
[21] *ILN*, May 29, 1920, *CW* 32:30.
[22] *The Well and the Shallows*, *CW* 3:501–2.

Carthage, where they threw their babies into the fire.[23] He predicted that abortion would be considered a sign of "progress".[24] He said that "our materialistic masters would put birth control into an immediate practical program" before anyone was even aware that it had happened,[25] and that it would be "applied to everybody and imposed by nobody".[26]

"The old parental authority", he said, would be swept away. Its place would be taken, "not by liberty or even licence, but by the far more sweeping and destructive authority of the State".[27] The State would become the only absolute in morals, so there would be "no appeal from it to God or man, to Christendom or conscience, to the individual or the family or the fellowship of all mankind".[28] We would then to try to use the government to remedy "the failures of all the families, all the nurseries, all the schools, all the workshops, all the secondary institutions that once had some authority of their own".[29] There would be rebellion, but the new rebels would not lay down rules, only exceptions.[30] And Chesterton said the one institution that he was sure would expand is the institution we call prison.[31]

Chesterton seemed to be writing for today when he said that the Christian was expected to praise every creed except his own.[32] He said that extremism is a fashionable term of

---

[23] *ILN*, August 7, 1926, *CW* 34:138–39.
[24] *The Well and the Shallows*, *CW* 3:530.
[25] *G.K.'s Weekly*, January 17, 1931.
[26] *Autobiography*, *CW* 16:330.
[27] *ILN*, November 24, 1928, *CW* 34:636.
[28] Ibid., December 21, 1918, *CW* 31:400.
[29] Ibid., March 24, 1923, *CW* 33:70.
[30] Ibid., August 29, 1931, *CW* 35:582.
[31] *Utopia of Usurers*, *CW* 5:427–28.
[32] *ILN*, August 11, 1928, *CW* 34:576.

reproach and any Christian who actually wanted to argue on behalf of his own faith is dismissed as an "extremist".

> The true religion of today does not concern itself with dogmas and doctrines. Indeed, it concerns itself almost entirely with diet.[33]

> Modern materialism ... is solemn about sports because it has no other rites to solemnise.[34]

> Many modern people have a sort of imaginative reverence for [the cinema] not only because a lot of money is got out of it, but merely because a lot of money is put into it.[35]

> Men in a state of decadence employ professionals to fight for them, professionals to dance for them, and a professional to rule them.[36]

The great Catholic apologist Frank Sheed, whose wife, Maisie Ward, wrote a biography of Chesterton, was one of many who marveled at the uncanny precision of Chesterton's predictions. And he said of Chesterton, "When a man is as right as that in his forecasts, there is some reason to think he may be right in his premises." [37]

And that is the important point, Chesterton was right in his premises. That is why he should be read and should be taught and should be studied. It is why, as we have noted, Étienne Gilson said Chesterton was one of the deepest thinkers who ever lived. "He was deep because he was right." [38]

---

[33] Ibid., May 11, 1929, *CW* 35:89.

[34] Ibid., November 15, 1930, *CW* 35:40.

[35] Ibid., October 8, 1921, *CW* 32:250.

[36] "Charles II", *Twelve Types* (London: Arthur L. Humphreys, 1903), 106.

[37] *The End of the Armistice* (compiler's note by Frank Sheed), *CW* 5:525.

[38] Quoted in Maisie Ward, *Gilbert Keith Chesterton* (New York: Sheed and Ward, 1942), 620.

Chesterton was right. He was right about both religion and politics. There are some who may agree with his religious writings but who would rather ignore his political ideas. There are others who read Chesterton only for his political ideas and do not care at all for his religious writings. But with Chesterton, you really cannot separate the two. For the same reason that truth and justice cannot be separated.

And while the two go together, Chesterton said that we do tend to make one mistake: we tend to make politics too important.

> We tend to forget how huge a part of a man's life is the same under a Sultan and a Senate, under Nero or St. Louis. Daybreak is a never-ending glory, getting out of bed is a never-ending nuisance; food and friends will be welcomed; work and strangers must be accepted and endured; birds will go bedwards and children won't, to the end of the last evening. And the worst peril is that in our just modern revolt against intolerable accidents we may have unsettled those things that alone make daily life tolerable. It will be an ironic tragedy if, when we have toiled to find rest, we find we are incurably restless. It will be sad if, when we have worked for our holiday, we find we have unlearnt everything but work. The typical modern man is the insane millionaire, who has drudged to get money, and then finds he cannot enjoy even money, but only drudgery. There is a danger that the social reformer may ... develop some of the madness of the millionaire whom he denounces. He may find that he has learnt how to build playgrounds, but forgotten how to play.[39]

Chesterton says there is only the Church and the world; there is nothing else. When it comes to the world, he reminds us

[39] "What Is Right with the World", *T.P.'s Weekly*, Christmas number, 1910; reprinted in the *Chesterton Review*, August-November 1990, 166.

that we have to hate it enough to want to change it, but love it enough to think it worth changing. Politics can get personal because of the intensity of that combination of love and hatred for the world. It is important to know that Chesterton defended patriotism as something perfectly natural. But once again, patriotism often means hating your country enough to want to change it, even while you love it enough to think it worth changing.

> The man who says, "My Country, right or wrong," is like the man who says "My mother, drunk or sober." [40]

Chesterton did not like representatives who did not represent or officials who put themselves above citizens rather than at their service or government that meddled in people's lives. He believed in democracy and defended democracy against any other form of government. But democracy is more than just voting, just as being a Christian is much more than just going to church. Democracy really means that the most important decisions must not be decided for people but must be left up to people to decide for themselves. Chesterton believed that the common man would act with common sense for the common good, but that his dignity and his freedom must be protected. He said that just as Christianity looks for the honest man inside the thief, democracy looks for the wise man inside the fool. And it encourages the fool to be wise.[41]

It is the snobs who insist on being foolish, with bizarre theories and unthinkable behavior. They attack common sense. Chesterton said that all of life's great questions should

---

[40] "A Defence of Patriotism", *The Defendant* (New York: Dodd, Mead, 1904), 125.

[41] *Charles Dickens, CW* 15:46.

be asked in words of one syllable—and answered in words of one syllable.[42] The snobs of the world avoid words of one syllable because they avoid common sense, plain words, clear thinking. They prefer long words, which are a substitute for thinking.[43]

And the one-syllable words that they most avoid are these: sin and faith. They do not want to face these simple, gigantic truths: that we have taken a good world and spoiled it. That we have to repent and return to the faith. Instead they attack the faith or ignore the faith or try to carry on without the faith.

In one of his typical paradoxes, Chesterton said sometimes a thing can be too big to be seen.[44] What the world can no longer see is that it was the Catholic Church that laid the foundation for Western civilization. The world has tried to push the Church aside, but, in the meantime, the world is still living off its Catholic capital.[45]

Only the Church can cure the ills that now face this civilization. Those who have abandoned the Church have in effect cut themselves off from something much greater than they realize. They cannot cure the ills. As Chesterton said:

The severed hand does not heal the whole body.[46]

But not only does the world stubbornly refuse the Church's help, some people even make themselves enemies of the Church and try to prevent it from having any influence in society. They try to discredit the Church by making all kinds

[42] *George Bernard Shaw, CW* 11:482.
[43] *ILN*, September 7, 1929, *CW* 35:160.
[44] *The Everlasting Man, CW* 2:163.
[45] *The Thing, CW* 3:147.
[46] *Chaucer, CW* 18:374.

of sensational charges against it. Chesterton shows how contradictory this is.

When people impute special vices to the Christian Church, they seem to entirely forget that the world (which is the only other thing there is) has these vices much more. The Church has been cruel; but the world has been much more cruel. The Church has plotted; but the world has plotted much more. The Church has been superstitious: but it has never been so superstitious as the world is when left to itself.[47]

Chesterton said that the earnest freethinkers, who are so worried about the persecutions of the past, are quite blind to what would happen in the world if their own ideas prevailed. In one of his most chilling prophecies he said:

Before the Liberal idea is dead or triumphant, we shall see wars and persecutions the like of which the world has never seen.[48]

Perhaps better than any other twentieth-century writer, Chesterton showed that the faith is the only thing that really makes sense. And though he wrote millions of words, he summed up his defense of the faith in only a few words:

The only argument against losing faith is that you also lose hope—and generally charity.[49]

Father Ian Boyd, the founder and editor of the *Chesterton Review*, made one of the most insightful observations about Chesterton when he said that Chesterton "never writes so profoundly about religion as when he is writing about

[47] *ILN*, December 14, 1907, *CW* 27:604.
[48] *Daily News*, February 18, 1905.
[49] *Hearst's Magazine*, January 1913.

something else".[50] Chesterton understood that Christianity is not confined only to what we do in church. It touches everything. It touches marriage and economics and literature and art and work and play and daydreams. Chesterton showed not only how reasonable the faith is, but also that it is the only thing that makes us fully functional. It is the only thing that can make us happy because it is connected to eternal happiness. This happiness filled G. K. Chesterton, filled him to overflowing. Chesterton was a complete thinker because his Catholic faith informed all of his thinking. That is why he is so consistent and so wondrously profound.

In this book, we have explored only twelve of Chesterton's books. He wrote dozens more. We have not looked at any of his novels or plays, his history and travel books, or his incomparable literary criticism, particularly his glorious writing on Charles Dickens. We have not looked at any of his wonderful poetry, which includes "The Donkey", a little poem that every schoolchild should memorize, and "The Ballad of the White Horse", an epic poem that every college student should study. And we have only scratched the surface of the thousands of essays he wrote, essays about everything and everything else.

Chesterton is big. He may be too big to get a hold of. He may be too big to be seen. But he is too big to be ignored.

I have tried to give him some of the attention he deserves, to bring his words to life. I have tried to introduce you to him, to give you the opportunity to get to know him. These first meetings have been far too brief. Hopefully, you will make yourself better acquainted with him by reading his books, many of which have been republished, and by read-

---

[50] "Chesterton Since His 100th Birthday", a talk given at the Eighteenth Annual Chesterton Conference, June 11, 1999, St. Paul, Minnesota.

ing periodicals, such as *Gilbert* Magazine and the *Chesterton Review*. Once you read Chesterton, you will find that you want to read more of him. And what will please you and astonish you is that he wrote so much that you probably will never read it all.

Various organizations such as the American Chesterton Society[51] have helped revive a widespread interest in this writer by attempting to get him taught in the schools again and by bringing his ideas back into the public arena.

Most of all, I would like to invite you simply to make friends with G. K. Chesterton, to laugh with him and have the pleasure of lifting a glass with him and sitting long at the table with him and all the giants of the faith. For that is a fellowship we were made for.

> We follow the feet
> Where all souls meet
> At the Inn at the end of the world.[52]

[51] The American Chesterton Society may be reached at
American Chesterton Society
4117 Pebblebrook Circle
Minneapolis, MN 55437
www.chesterton.org

[52] "A Child of the Snows", *The Collected Poems of G. K. Chesterton* (New York: Dodd, Mead, 1949), 141.